I0715892

Scorched Redemption
The Sendaxa Chronicles, Book 2

By

REBECCA HEFNER

This book is a work of fiction. Names, characters, places and incidents are the product of the author's imagination and are used fictitiously. Any resemblance to actual events, locales or persons, living or dead, is coincidental.

Copyright © 2024 by Rebecca Hefner. All rights reserved, including the right to reproduce, distribute or transmit in any form or by any means.

Cover Design: The Book Brander
Editor: Megan McKeever
Proofreader: Nay's Notations – Editing and Proofreading Services

Contents

For everyone like Arianna who's given up on love. May your Dominic come along and open his heart just for you...

Chapter 1

Sometime in the not-so-distant future...

Dominic Cavalleri gasped before jerking upright and placing his hand over his heart. The organ threatened to beat out of his chest as he glared at the woman at the foot of the bed. Arianna Lawson stood tall, banging a spoon on a pan as she yelled, "Rise and shine!"

"Jesus, Ari," he said, clutching his pec. "Are you *trying* to give me a heart attack?"

"You're not very good at dying," she said, planting the fist with the spoon on her hip. "So I think your ticker's just fine."

Releasing a breath, he ran a hand over his short hair. "I was shot three weeks ago, in case you don't remember. My body's still recovering."

"Tell it to someone who cares, old man." Striding forward, she cocked a brow. "It's time to train. Since you did five miles yesterday, we're going to run seven today. And then, target practice."

"Fucking drill sergeant," Dominic muttered, lifting the covers on the medical stretcher that doubled as his bed. When his feet touched the floor, he stood—slowly, so he didn't lose his balance.

"Best drill sergeant you'll ever have," she muttered, eyeing him warily. "You okay? Don't faint on me."

"I'm good." Dominic touched the laceration at the juncture of his neck and shoulder. Thankfully, Dr. Danica Lawson-Ward, Arianna's sister, had been nursing the wound, and it was healing nicely. Although their mission to retrieve the EverLife antidote had been messy, it had been success-ful—and Dani was now hard at work trying to replicate it.

"I just need to clean the abrasion and wash off," Dominic said, grateful the abandoned school they were inhabiting now had running water. The compound's leader, Arthur Reyes, had tasked some former contractors and plumbers with restoring the plumbing from a nearby well. It certainly made things easier in their dystopian world.

"I'll be by the front door in ten minutes. Don't make me wait. I've got shit to do today." Pivoting, she thrust her chin in the air and stalked from the room.

"Infuriating woman." Dominic headed to the bathroom, complete with stalls and functional sinks. After rinsing off and cleaning his wound, he applied a fresh bandage before throwing on some of the sweats Reyes's men had given him. After tying his sneakers, which had lasted surprisingly long in their dystopian world, he went in search of his training partner.

"About time," Arianna said, pushing the door open and ushering him outside.

Dominic squinted at the bright sun, wishing he still owned trivial things like sunglasses. Before the world end-ed, small luxuries were easily taken for granted. Now, hu-manity existed in a fragile balance between survival and extinction. Only time would tell which path they would take.

"I figured we'd jog to the outer wall and do some laps," Arianna said, planting her feet wide and bending over to stretch. She moved from side to side, and Dominic had to squelch the urge to look at her breasts as the neckline of her shirt bared her cleavage. Her firm ass stuck high in the air, and he licked his lips, suddenly longing to place his palms on the smooth skin...

"Earth to Dom," she said, rising. "Ready?"

Nodding, he did a few stretches before falling into step beside her. They jogged at a quick, no-nonsense pace, and he inhaled the warm air into his lungs. It was almost September, and soon the leaves would begin to turn, but for now, he basked in the heady late-summer breeze.

Every so often, he glanced at Arianna, acknowledging how lucky he was to have her as his training partner. She'd been an excellent soldier and high-ranking officer in the US Army before she'd retired to pursue her own security business. The world had fallen apart, so she hadn't been able to fulfill that dream. Protecting her sisters and saving humanity had become her new calling, and she excelled at it.

When Dominic first met Arianna, he'd made the mistake of judging her like many others did. As someone who was harsh and unyielding. And yes, Arianna Lawson definitely had those qualities.

But as he got to know her, he began to see the gruffness for what it was: a shield to guard herself from getting hurt. Arianna had always been a protector and safeguarded herself since no one had ever thought to protect her. The stern, uncompromising woman who didn't appear to need anyone.

Dominic had been drawn to Danica, who was much more open and trusting. Through the shared grief of losing her mother and Dominic's sister to cancer, they'd formed an intimate bond.

Dani helped Dominic cope with the deaths of his family members, which were both tragic and senseless. His parents had been murdered during a robbery at their Washington, DC, home. Although the perpetrators were eventually caught and sent to prison, that outcome offered little solace to Dominic.

And then, barely a year later, his sister, Pam, was diagnosed with stage-four cancer. When most of her friends were celebrating their twenty-first birthdays by tossing back their first drinks, she'd succumbed to the deadly disease, leaving him alone in a world comprised of pain and heartache.

Dominic had been left scarred—both mentally and physically—since he carried a nasty scar from his Middle East deployment almost two decades ago. Courtesy of an overzealous rebel soldier with a machete, the jagged laceration ran from the outer corner of his eyebrow, across his nose, and ended at the opposite corner of his lips.

The pain from that scar had been temporary, although he'd wear it for the rest of his life. The agony from the loss of his family was an invisible wound he carried inside, deep within the heart he'd shut down long ago.

Danica had been the one exception. Since she was married to his best friend, Dominic knew loving her was safe—that he would never act on it since she adored Maverick. It allowed Dominic to imagine he still had the ability to feel *some* sliver of emotion.

And that's where he and Arianna were *exactly* alike.

Because his love for Dani had been a shield. One to protect him from ever again experiencing the pain he felt when his parents and sister died.

Dominic had convinced himself to love someone unavailable so he wouldn't get hurt.

Arianna had just given up on love completely. They were two broken souls rotating in the same orbit.

Getting shot was the wake-up call Dominic needed. He realized it was time to stop romanticizing something that wasn't real. If his soul hadn't been broken, he might have stopped to appreciate what was right in front of him. If anyone was a match for Dominic, it was Arianna. The stoic, fierce woman who pretended not to care.

He would admit she was a good actress. He hadn't seen any indication of her true feelings. Not until he was bleeding out on the cold laboratory floor, holding his neck as she begged him not to die.

In that moment, Dominic had seen every ounce of emotion the woman kept bottled inside. Her gorgeous hazel eyes had swirled with pleading, longing and...*love*. Dominic was no expert at emotion, but he couldn't deny the intensity that passed between them in that moment.

The moment he'd realized he might actually be ready to try and love someone again. That it might be worth the risk if it was *her*.

"Stop staring at me," she droned, the words breathy as she jogged. "And if you look at my tits again, I'll break your kneecaps."

Dominic pursed his lips, silently admitting he'd stolen a glance or two at her breasts as she jogged. They were small but perfectly proportioned for her strong, tall body, and he suddenly wondered how well they would fit in his palms. Glancing down, he imagined cupping one with his hand and trailing his thumb over her nipple. Would she moan with desire or punch him in the face if he tried? Hell, she'd probably do both, but he figured suffering through the latter was worth it for the pleasure he'd experience from the former.

"What are you smirking at?" she asked, jogging to the high metal wall before stopping and bending over to catch her breath. "Let's take a breather before we begin the laps."

Dominic used the break to stretch, his body still sore from the injury. Swinging his tattooed arms around in large circles, he relished the ache in his healing muscles. He was recovering well—thanks in part to Arianna's ceaseless efforts to train with him—but stopping to stretch was a good call. At forty-one, he was no spring chicken, and knew that constant movement was essential for increasing blood flow and ensuring his muscles didn't cramp.

"I'm laughing at how you can't help yourself. You love busting my balls, Ari."

"You make it easy," she said with a shrug. "And I told you not to call me that."

"I think the habit's formed, sweetheart. Sorry—"

Arianna gripped his jaw, quick as lightning, and squeezed. It hurt like hell, but she didn't punch him in his wound, so he figured he'd take the win. If she really wanted to hurt him, that's where she'd aim, and they both knew it.

"And you definitely don't want to call me *that*," she warned, her fingers tightening against his stubble. Her glare was fierce, her almost-six-foot frame imposing even though he was half a foot taller. "I demoted men for calling me that back in the day."

Ever so slowly, Dominic slid his palm over the silken skin of her wrist. "Message received." Tugging her hand from his jaw, he held fast when she tried to pull away.

"Hey!"

"I'm not one of your subordinates, Arianna," he said, careful to use her full name so she wouldn't focus on something trivial. In truth, her nickname suited her, and he doubted it bothered her when he used it. But it was something else to hide behind. Another defense she could use to pretend she hated him.

"I know that," she said, attempting to yank her wrist from his grasp. "Dom—"

"Stick your hand in the rattlesnake's den and you're going to get bitten." He released her, a bit breathless from the feel of her skin against his palm.

Her cheeks flushed under her half-shaven head as angry eyes studied him under long, dark lashes.

"I'm not scared of you, Arianna."

A puff of air exited her lungs as her expression became confused. "I know. That's one of the things I like most about you. You're able to put up with my shit."

Dominic smiled at the concession, which he rarely experienced with her. "I didn't think you liked anything about me," he softly teased.

"That's the *only* thing," she said, her tone acerbic as she backed away. Her long fingers rubbed her wrist as she studied him, and he wondered if she mourned the loss of his skin against hers too. "Come on. Break's over. We need to get your heart rate back up."

Frustration set in as she retreated behind her shell. Aching to say something before the mask fully returned, he stepped forward. Her muscles stiffened, but she stood her ground, spine straightening as she gazed up at him. He towered over her, his broad shoulders tense in anticipation of the conversation they needed to have. Neither of them had acknowledged what happened in the squalid laboratory hallway when he was shot, and he felt it was time.

"Are we going to talk about what happened at the lab?"

A challenge entered her gaze, and admiration swelled at her pride. Arianna was confident and sure of herself, and damn, it was attractive. Not only did it set his body on fire, but he had a sneaking suspicion she let it go in the bedroom. That when she found the right partner, she would open herself up and let him take control.

And lord help him, but he wanted to be that man.

"There's nothing to talk about. You survived and Dani got the serum. The woman you love is safe, and we've moved on to Phase II of our plan."

Dominic's eyes narrowed as he battled to keep the frustration at bay. Although he loved verbally sparring with her, dismissing their feelings was beneath them both. If she wouldn't admit them, at least he could.

"You know my feelings for Dani were...something born from mutual experience," he said, shaking his head.

"Of course." Stepping back, she raised her arms in a stretch before kicking both legs to reinvigorate them. "I mean, everyone loves Dani. Makes complete sense. Let's go. I've got practice with the kids in an hour."

She turned and began jogging beside the metallic wall that surrounded the compound. Smiling at the fact he'd been thoroughly dismissed, he jolted into a sprint to catch up with her. Arianna had been a premier athlete in college and had led her team to the college softball tournament. When she'd discovered the kids in the compound had organized a makeshift wiffle ball league, she'd offered to coach them.

Chris, one of the children who'd helped acclimate them to the abandoned school, lit up at her offer. She'd been coaching them for two weeks on the grown-over baseball diamond behind the school. Dominic thought it spoke volumes about her character. She could pretend to be a heartless grump all day long, but the woman was selfless in every way.

And she deserved to be loved that way in return.

As Dominic's feet moved in tandem with hers, he stole another glance out of the corner of his eye. Her skin glistened with a sheen of sweat, and he envisioned licking it away as she moaned his name...

He'd been a blind idiot with her for far too long. Thankfully, the universe had decided it wasn't his time yet. He'd survived a near-fatal blow, and he wouldn't squander the opportunity to do things differently this time.

This time, he would break down Arianna's walls, even if she fought him the entire way.

And when he succeeded, perhaps they would finally experience the profound emotion they were both so terrified to feel.

Perhaps, together, they could learn to love without pain.

Inhaling the fragrant air, Dominic ran beside the woman who consumed his thoughts, determined to make it happen.

Chapter 2

Arianna Lawson placed two fingers between her lips and gave a loud whistle. "Okay, boys. That's enough for today. Head back to home plate."

Several kids ran from the outfield as she placed her hand on the catcher's shoulder. "Nice job, Chris. You're getting quicker at popping up from the catcher's position. I can tell you've been practicing."

White teeth flashed under his thick mop of brown hair. "Thanks, Arianna. I wanted to pitch, but no one told me being a catcher was so fun."

"Pitchers get all the glory, but catchers are the anchor. You're a natural leader, and you're good at anchoring the other kids."

He beamed under her praise as the children surrounded them.

"Great job today, guys," she said, clapping her hands in a few solid claps. "I might be leaving on a mission soon, and when I go, I'm leaving Chris in charge. I want you all to keep practicing, okay?"

"Yes, ma'am," they chimed.

Arianna smiled, remembering the days when grown men had addressed her that way. Times had changed, but she still enjoyed the thrill of leading a team. Even if they were a bunch of kids learning to play wiffle ball.

Splaying her hand above the ground, palm down, she waited until they'd all rested their smaller hands atop hers. "Gooooo, team!"

They raised their hands in a simultaneous cheer before gathering their tattered gloves and balls to head home.

"Well, Ari. It seems you've already got the 'mom' thing down pat," Dani said, smiling broadly as she approached.

"They're cute," she responded with a shrug. "What can I say? I was doomed the first time they asked me to play with them. Adorable little bastards."

Chuckling, Dani crossed her arms over her chest to ward off the chill. Although the morning had been warm, a cold front seemed to be moving in. Glancing toward the rapidly darkening sky, Arianna jerked her head. "Come on. Let's head back to the school before it rains."

Nodding, Dani slid her arm around Arianna's waist, the gesture representative of her caring nature. Arianna wasn't overly affectionate—to put it mildly—but they'd been through some pretty rough shit lately, and she loved her sister immensely. Placing her arm over Dani's shoulders, they walked silently as the gravity of their current situation loomed between them.

"We have to go get her, Ari," Dani said softly, concern in her green eyes as she glanced up at Arianna. "Raquel fucked up royally, but we can't leave her with Cromwell. Whether she believes it or not, she's in danger."

"I know." Anger hummed deep within as Arianna contemplated Raquel's betrayal. They'd both trusted their little sister, never understanding she posed a grave threat.

Raquel blamed Dani for denying her a proper goodbye when their mother died from cancer. In a twisted act of revenge for that supposed misdeed, she'd betrayed them all. Raquel had been responsible for the blow that caused Dani's amnesia. Now, she was living in the DC Sen City controlled by Luthor Cromwell, the notorious man who'd funded the drug that destroyed society and created their dystopian world.

Sadly, Dani had been the scientist who created the drug, although she'd been an unwitting pawn. Now that they'd retrieved the antidote from the Sendaxa lab in Maryland, Dani was intent on creating a remedy to battle the EverLife addiction that crippled so many.

Curing humanity would mean defeating Luthor Cromwell, who now commanded what remained of the US military—and also the man who was harboring Raquel in exchange for her extensive knowledge as a botanist. Her expertise could be used to create more addictive drugs and extend Luthor's domination of their broken society. Arianna loved her two sisters, and vacillated between heartbreak and fury at Raquel's betrayal. No matter how angry Raquel was, deceiving your family was a concept Arianna would never understand.

"You need to keep working on replicating the antidote, so I'll go to the DC Sen City and get Raquel," Arianna said.

"It's dangerous—"

"Yeah? Thanks for the heads up."

Breathing a laugh, Dani sighed. "I can't lose you too. I'll only feel comfortable if Maverick and Dom go with you."

"No fucking way. I don't need a babysitter. I can rescue her myself. You need Maverick here. He's formed an alliance with Reyes, and you need a trained soldier to remain behind. The people here have been good to us so far, but that could change anytime. I won't leave you unprotected."

Stopping, Dani pulled away and turned to face her. Placing her hands in her back pockets, she kicked the ground with the toe of her sneaker. "Then I guess Dom will have to go with you. Do you think he's ready?"

Arianna's lips thinned. "I don't need him. I can do it myself—"

"That's not what I asked," she said, softly but firmly. "Do you think he's healed enough to go with you?"

Arianna's lips fluttered as she crossed her arms. "Probably. He didn't croak when we ran seven miles this morning."

Dani pursed her lips, obviously trying to contain her smile as Arianna rolled her eyes.

"This isn't some grand love story, Dani. I told you, I don't want that shit. I want you to save the world so I can get away from people, not form *more* relationships. Stop trying to matchmake or whatever the fuck you're doing."

Her sister's eyes darted between hers as silence stretched between them. Finally, she stated the truth. "He knows how you feel. Why are you pretending you don't care?"

"He doesn't know shit," she said, kicking the ground. "And he loves you—"

"No," she said, showing her palm. "I'm not letting you hide behind that anymore, Ari. I have lots of notes in my journal to remind you that you deserve love and to stop pushing it away." She flashed a cheeky grin. "And Dominic's a good match for you. The whole sexy scar thing," she pointed at her face, indicating where Dominic's scar resided, "plus the way he looks at you when he thinks no one is watching... It's really cute."

"I'm banning you from writing about me in your journal. It's annoying."

Dani bit her bottom lip to contain her smile. "Sorry, but I need my notes to remember what the hell I'm doing. I'm getting more flashes of memory back every day, but I'm nowhere near one hundred percent." She patted Arianna's upper arm affectionately. "And you're one of my favorite people to write about, so you're staying in."

Releasing a frustrated breath, Arianna ran a hand over the silky dark hair that covered half of her head. "Fine, but a discussion about Dominic is off the table. It doesn't matter anyway. I have one objective: to help you save the world. I know you won't be able to fully concentrate on doing that until Raquel is safe. Even though you're pissed, you don't want her dead. So, I'll go to Washington, DC, and get her. Alone."

Dani squinted one eye as she contemplated. "You know, even if I agree, Dominic won't let you go alone. He'll insist on going with you, especially if Mav stays here with me."

"Doesn't matter. I'll leave when he's sleeping."

Emitting a resigned laugh, Dani stretched out her hands. Arianna took them and held tight.

"You know I want you to be happy, right?" Dani whispered, her eyes filling with tears as her voice tuned raspy. "I hate that you fight being happy, Arianna. Mom would want more for you."

"I'll get what I want when you replicate the antidote," she said, squeezing Dani's fingers. "I'll finally get to have a kid and live off the grid where I can get some peace and quiet."

Dani's eyebrows lifted as excitement laced her expression. "Dom's kid?"

Laughing, Arianna tugged her sister against her side as they resumed walking. "Everyone always says I'm the stubborn one, but I don't hold a candle to you."

"Truth."

They walked arm in arm until they reached the school that was their makeshift home. "Once I'm done in the lab, I'm going to make dinner in the old home economics room. We can discuss your mission to retrieve Raquel while we eat."

"Fine."

"Okay, I've got to get back to work," Dani said, waving as she backed down the hallway toward the old sixth grade science lab. "I'm getting closer, Ari."

"It's been three weeks. Give yourself some grace. I know you can do it."

Her sister nodded before turning and striding away.

Arianna entered the bathroom, which had stalls and rows of mirrors above functional sinks. After washing off the grime of the day, she trailed to the gymnasium, intent on getting in one more workout before dinner. If she was going to rescue her sister, she'd need to be fit and ready.

Especially if Dominic came with her.

Frowning, she debated the pros and cons of having him by her side. He wasn't in prime condition since being shot, but the man was recovering like some kind of cyborg. Whatever physical limitations he had wouldn't hinder him.

But having him near her might compromise her mission. After all, it was hard to continue to pretend indifference when he was around all the damn time.

And Arianna was intent on remaining indifferent.

She'd played the love game before, several times in her life. Each time, she'd been badly burned. Each man had tossed her love back in her face as if it were trash flitting along a filthy street.

If she allowed Dominic in and he ultimately rejected her, she wasn't sure she'd survive. After all, she loved the man to the point of distraction. It was utterly ridiculous and completely uncontrollable.

And he'd already rejected her countless times anyway. Every time he gazed longingly at Dani when Arianna had been there. Every time he looked past her to see someone he truly *wanted* to see.

No one had ever wanted to see her. And damn it, she was tired of caring or wanting them to try. Smart people eventually stopped doing the same shit and expecting different results. And she wasn't a genius like Dani, but she was pretty fucking smart.

Although Dani was her adopted sister, they shared a bond more solid than blood. Arianna's birth parents had died in a car accident when she was only four years old, and Cynthia Lawson had adopted her even though she was young and most likely unprepared for a child.

Arianna loved Dani from the first moment she felt her kick beneath Cynthia's swollen belly. They grew up as sisters and confidants before eventually experiencing the death of Dani's father, Bill, and the immeasurable heartache of Cynthia's death from cancer.

So much fucking loss. If Arianna took the time to dwell on it, she'd probably drown in grief.

Grief and loss...and *pain*...had no place in their dystopian world.

Picking up the dumbbells, Arianna began to furiously pump, working her biceps as she stared into the faded mirror. Gazing into her own eyes, she vowed to keep the wall between her and Dominic Cavalleri firmly in place.

Because if she let her guard down and he decided to discard her as thoughtlessly as every man had in the past—or leave her as most of the people she'd ever loved eventually did—it might break her.

Observing him love Dani reaffirmed that emotional connection wasn't in the cards for her. Allowing Dominic inside only to lose him as she'd lost everyone else wasn't an option.

She'd survived losing her adoptive mother and her sister's betrayal.

Hell, she'd survived the end of civilization as they'd known it.

But Arianna knew she wasn't strong enough to survive gaining—and then losing—the love of her fucking life.

So, she would push him away and hope the stubborn man got the message.

Arianna Lawson's heart was closed for business, and she didn't plan on opening it ever again.

Chapter 3

D r. Danica Lawson-Ward gazed into the microscope, absently murmuring to herself as she studied the liquid specimen on the slide.

"The cyclotides are working," she whispered excitedly. "Holy shit!"

"Am I going to get fired if I don't know what cyclotides are?" a deep voice asked in her ear.

Smiling, she glanced up at her husband as his arms encircled her from behind. "I think I'll let you live. And do you work for me anyway? I think you work for Reyes, whether you want to admit it or not."

Maverick's lips curved. "For a guy I was going to murder the first time I met him, he's turned out to be pretty cool."

Breathing a laugh, Dani turned and slid her arms around his neck. "You're basically his second-in-command at this point."

His features tensed as he nodded. "Although I detest the thought of more fighting and destruction, we're going to have to protect ourselves if we want to distribute your formula to the masses. And we'll eventually have to take the offensive. We need to be prepared and I like being on the inside."

"As long as you protect yourself first," she said, tightening her arms. "I just barely remembered who you are. I need to make up for lost time."

"Any new memories today?" he asked, tapping her forehead.

"Did we take a vacation to Peru?" She squinted one eye as a vague memory appeared at the edge of her consciousness.

"Yep. You complained the entire time we hiked to the top of Machu Pichu, but once we got there, it was breathtaking."

"I'm sure I did no such thing!"

Chuckling, he brushed her nose with his. "You did, but your expression when we finally made it was worth it." Stealing a kiss, he nipped her lip. "I'm happy you remember."

"I remember some of it," she said, pecking his lips before releasing him. "But not enough. It's frustrating as hell, but I'm trying not to waste energy on things I can't control."

Craning his neck, he glanced at the microscope. "How's the new antidote coming along?"

"Good." Pointing to her scribbled notes, her finger slowly ran across the page as she spoke. "The original antidote we retrieved from the lab was mostly comprised of plant and herbs. It's as if I knew I might need to reproduce it outside of a lab with elements commonly found in nature."

"My wife, the genius," he said reverently. "You knew Luthor was bad news toward the end, so that doesn't surprise me."

Dani glowed at his praise, his support a stabilizing presence against the turmoil that swam deep in her gut. Although she'd awoken with barely any memory of the past five years, she'd felt safe with him from the first moment she opened her eyes. It didn't make sense to her logical, scientific brain, but she couldn't deny the tangible energy that connected her to Maverick.

Returning to the topic, she continued. "I'm trying to rebuild the antidote with naturally occurring plant elements so we can mass produce it. I'm also attempting to create something that's also a cure, so it's challenging."

Maverick cocked his brow. "But you love a challenge."

"Damn right I do," she said with a firm nod. "I'm close, Mav, and I'm determined to create an antidote that's even more effective than the one I created in the lab."

"So, tell me about cyclotides."

Blowing out a breath, she hesitated as she tried to explain in layman's terms. "Cyclotides are organic peptides found in violets and pansies that bond with opioid receptors. In theory, if injected into the blood stream, cyclotides can bond with the receptors first so EverLife never has a chance to induce the high that leads to addiction."

His eyebrows lifted. "So, they could be preventative?"

"Yes. But I also want to include compounds that will reverse cravings for anyone already addicted. The plants I've identified that work the best so far are milk thistle, St. John's Wart, ginger and cayenne pepper."

"Cayenne pepper?"

"It's a potent provitamin. If I can get all the elements combined in the right portions, it just might work."

"Sadly, there are almost fifty subjects for you to practice on in the clinic."

The clinic was a run-down regional hospital that had been abandoned when society collapsed. It sat inside the compound's walls and had two generators that allowed it to function as a care facility—barely. Former nurses and physicians volunteered to help the addicted and sick, and Dani would eventually test her new formula on the patients there.

"I have no doubt you'll knock it out of the park," he said, reassuringly squeezing her shoulder. "What can I do to help?"

"I need a team to scout for the various plants so I can add them to the garden behind the school. Some of them already grow here naturally, but others will require scouting beyond the compound. I wish Raquel was here so she could help me. She knows more about plants than anyone."

"I know," he said, his tone sympathetic as he shook his head. "Such a damn shame. I'm no expert, but I can try and scout for you."

"I'll just need your protection as we search outside the walls. I should be able to find everything I need if we dedicate the time to looking."

"Of course." His eyes darted between hers. "But if I'm protecting you, that means I can't go with Arianna to rescue Raquel."

"Dom's going to go with her. We spoke about it this afternoon."

"And she agreed?"

"She, uh…" Clearing her throat, Dani shrugged. "I'm not actually sure, but I'm putting my foot down. Ari's tough, but there's no way she's going to DC by herself. End of story."

"There's my slugger," he said, flashing a grin. "And Dom's ready to travel?"

"I've been treating his wound, but it's healing better than I could've hoped. I don't see it hindering him."

"And are we sure Arianna won't strangle him?" he teased.

"I'm hoping they'll tangle in other ways, if you catch my drift." She waggled her eyebrows.

Maverick's expression warmed as he studied her. "My optimistic scientist. I hope it happens."

"On that note, I need to finish my notes before I cook dinner. It will probably get a bit explosive when I insist on Dom accompanying her. I need to prepare."

"You've got this," he said, kissing her forehead. "Need help?"

"Can you get a pot of water boiling? I found a box of pasta and a jar of sauce in one of the cabinets in the home economics room, so we're having spaghetti. I'll be there shortly."

Nodding, he winked before pivoting and heading out the door. Tilting her head, Dani observed his firm ass and broad shoulders, the corner of her mouth ticking up as she inwardly squealed with the zeal of a teenage girl.

"God, he's hot," she breathed before turning back to the microscope to get to work. After logging the rest of the session notes, she capitulated to her growling stomach and headed to cook dinner.

Chapter 4

An hour later, Arianna entered the home economics room, mouth watering at the decadent smell. Approaching Dani at the stove, she inhaled deeply.

"I forgot how good pasta smells. Yum."

"Since we have to divide it into five servings, I also made a salad for everyone. It won't be a huge meal, but the spinach growing in the garden out back is fresh and we need veggies."

"Why do we need five servings—?"

"Because you have an extra guest," Arthur Reyes's deep voice chimed as he breezed into the room. Arching a brow, he gestured toward Dani. "She invited me."

"We're going to discuss your trip to retrieve Raquel, and Arthur has all the cars since he's in charge of the compound," Dani said, her expression laced with a twinge of guilt at the omission as she shrugged. "It's better if we strategize together."

Arianna's gaze raked over Arthur. He'd been kind to them so far, but she was skeptical of everyone in their post-apocalyptic world. Arthur Reyes had been speculating a run for president before society fell apart, and she sometimes wondered if his motives were pure. Did he truly want to help rebuild the world, or did he want to replace Luthor Cromwell and seize ultimate power himself?

"I like that she doesn't trust me," Arthur said, annoying Arianna as he referred to her as if she wasn't in the room. "It keeps me honest."

"Honesty isn't really what I'm worried about," Arianna muttered, picking up two of the salad plates and setting them on the table Dani had set for dinner. "I'm just wary of egomaniacs who want to rule the world."

"All the more reason to take down Cromwell," Arthur said with a thoughtful nod.

Arianna just grunted as she continued placing food on the table. Dominic and Maverick strolled into the room, and Dani turned off the stove.

"Grab it while it's hot, guys," she said, waving them over.

Arianna served herself a fifth of the noodles and sauce, careful to only take her share so everyone had an equal portion. Once they were seated, Maverick smiled at Dominic.

"How are you feeling today, man?"

"Good. Arianna pushed me on our run this morning, but it was exactly what I needed." Rubbing the bandage over his wound, he smiled. "It's just an annoying gash at this point. It alternates between slightly stinging and itching ever since Dani remove the stitches."

"Thank god the bullet didn't hit a major vessel," Maverick said. "You were really lucky."

As they spoke, Arianna recalled the moment when Dominic had been sprawled before her, blood gushing from his neck as he struggled to breathe. It had been one of the most terrifying moments of her life. She'd begged every god she didn't believe in to save him—even if he was in love with Dani and would never love her back.

His words from their jog resurfaced, causing her to form a slight scowl. "*You know my feelings for Dani were born from mutual experience.*" Inwardly scoffing, Arianna bristled. He could deny it, but she'd seen his feelings for Dani on full display more times than she could count. He was gentle with her. Soft. Compassionate. Everything one should be for someone they loved...

"Ari?" Dani asked.

"Huh?"

"You zoned out there for a second," she teased. "I was telling Arthur that you agreed to go to DC to retrieve Raquel."

"Uh, yeah," she said, running her palm over the nearly bald side of her head. "I've started growing this out so I won't stand out as much. Being almost six feet tall with broad shoulders is already noticeable enough, but I'd like to try and be inconspicuous as I infiltrate the city. Not an easy feat."

"And I told Maverick that you agreed Dom should come with you," Dani continued, her tone firm. "That way, Mav can stay here and help us at the compound."

Arianna's expression turned deadpan. "I agreed to no such thing. Dom needs to recover. I'm going alone."

"No fucking way," Dominic said, his tone low and immobile. "I'm coming with you."

"I don't have time to play nurse—"

"I'm well enough to help you, Ari," Dominic interrupted, annoying her with his bossy tone. "And our chances are better if we work together."

"I know I'm new to the inner circle," Arthur said, showing his palms, "but I agree. And I think you two could actually complete *two* missions while you're there."

Arianna stared at the ceiling in frustration. "Oh, great. Another man's opinion I don't need. I'm all ears."

"Ari..." Dani warned.

Arianna just glared at her as Arthur continued.

"I understand that rescuing Raquel is important to you. I'd like to say I wouldn't have the same deference for a traitor, but if it were my sister, I'd probably go through the depths of hell to save her, even if she betrayed me."

"We're both pissed and heartbroken," Dani said, her shoulders deflating as she shook her head. "But she's our sister and we promised our mom we'd take care of her."

With a compassionate nod, Arthur continued. "As you all know, I have a well-trained team of spies who are excellent at obtaining information from DC. All signs indicate a rebellion is brewing inside the city walls."

"Tristan Holder indicated the same to me when we spoke in the lab," Arianna confirmed.

"I'm aware. Knowing this, I'd like to ask you to approach Tristan when you're in the city. It seems he's playing both sides of the fence, considering that he let you live during the lab break in, and I want to see if we can pull him to our side."

"To what end?" Arianna asked.

Sitting back, Arthur thoughtfully rubbed his chin. "I want an ally on the inside. Once Dani has a working antidote, we're going to eventually storm the city. It will be easier to take Cromwell down if we work with someone from his inner circle, especially if a rebellion is already forming. I would bet that Tristan is involved."

Arianna chewed as she mulled. Considering Tristan's actions at the lab, it was possible they could form an alliance. "I don't trust him, but I think you're right. He's certainly not Cromwell's biggest fan."

"If you can make contact with him, I have a secret radio channel set up between our compound and several others. We'll loop him in and hopefully work with him to formulate a plan to infiltrate DC. It's time we took it back for the people."

"And who will lead them then?" Arianna asked derisively. "You?"

Arthur's eyes flared with equal parts mirth and annoyance as he smirked. "Perhaps. I've done a pretty good job running this place. The sick and addicted are treated well in the clinic by volunteers. Children who lost parents are taken in by adults who want to help. We're a highly functioning compound considering the state of the world and lack of resources."

Arianna studied Maverick and Dani as she contemplated. "You two okay with this?"

"If it's not Reyes, it will be someone else," Maverick said, resignation in his voice. "Better to go with the devil we know—"

"Hey," Arthur interrupted, cupping Maverick's shoulder, "am I the devil in this situation?"

Grinning, Maverick shrugged. "I think so. But you've given us shelter and your actions have been honorable." Looking at Arianna, he arched a brow. "I trust him, Ari."

"To be clear, I'll need a competent, trustworthy leadership team if we successfully wrest power from Cromwell," Arthur said, lifting a finger. "I want you on that team, Maverick. Maybe that will help ease your concerns, Arianna. Someone you trust will be nearby to keep me in check."

Arianna's eyes narrowed. "I thought you two were ready to settle down and have a bunch of babies once Dani healed everyone."

"I've got a few good years left in me and I think we can do both." Maverick slid his fingers over Dani's wrist and gave a gentle squeeze. "And I want to help. Rebuilding the world is going to be hard enough. Might as well finish the job we started."

Swallowing the last of her pasta, Arianna pushed the plate away and rested her chin on her hand. Her lips fluttered as she expelled a breath, causing the hair above her forehead to flit. "Fine. If Mav's involved in your regime, I'm in. But first, Dani has to finish the antidote and we have to take back the city."

"I've already got a team ready to scour the forest until we find the rest of the plants and herbs I need. I'm close to having some compounds I can test on the addicted clinic patients."

"Thank god," Arthur said. "We keep them alive with the shitty antidotes we get from black-market dealers, but they're full of dangerous chemicals. We need your pure antidote, Dani."

Arianna found his tone sincere and made a silent note to ease up on him. Saving lives was a worthy endeavor, and she wanted to do her part. "I'll approach Tristan while I'm in the city, and I have some old contacts I can try and track down to get information on a possible rebellion. Not sure if they're still in DC, but it's worth a shot. I'll need all the details on the secret radio channel so I pass on the correct intel to Tristan."

"*We'll* approach Tristan and Arianna's contacts," Dominic corrected as Arianna scowled. "And I'd like a full briefing too."

"I'll brief you both in the morning, if that works," Arthur said, rising. "Meet me at the abandoned gas station down the road from the school. After the briefing, we can pick out a car for you to drive to DC." Facing Dani, he gave a slight bow. "Dinner was lovely, thank you. Do you need me to help clean up?"

"No, I'll do it," she said, waving her hand. "Washing dishes is cathartic for me. I need some mindless activity after stressing my brain all day."

With a polite nod, he waved to everyone before departing.

Arianna threaded her hands behind her head, studying everyone as they finished dinner.

"Rescue Raquel, get Tristan on our side, and figure out if a rebellion is forming. Piece of cake."

Dominic shot her an acerbic look, understanding the mission would be extremely complex. "The city is heavily fortified, but I know it well since I used to live there. We'll need to find a place to stay that takes cash and stay off the grid."

The legs of Arianna's chair scraped across the floor as she stood. "I lived there too," she said, already frustrated that he was making decisions for her. Approaching him, she glared down as she lowered her voice. "And let's get one thing straight. *I'm* the leader of this mission. You can come with me, but I give the orders." Without waiting for a response, she strolled out of the room.

Chapter 5

D ominic pursed his lips at Arianna's departing figure. Glancing between Maverick and Dani, he grinned. "She seems thrilled I'm going with her."

Tossing back her head, Dani broke into a laugh. "Ah, Dom. Thank god you're not easily intimidated. She's my sister and I adore her, but damn, she's scary sometimes."

Chuckling, Dominic regarded the woman he'd convinced himself he loved for years. He still carried unwavering affection for Dani, but something had changed when he'd been shot. Visions of Arianna's multicolored eyes brimming with tears as she silently begged him not to die flashed in his brain, and he remembered the full force of the buzzing energy that always vibrated between them. It was much more powerful than anything he'd felt for Dani, and he cursed himself that he'd overlooked it for so long.

"Is it weird that I like how intimidating she is?"

Dani's smile widened into a full-on beam. "Nope. It's about time someone did."

Affection swelled at her obvious love for her sister as he stood. "I'm going to talk to her. She'll be fine, and I won't let anything happen to her."

"I know you won't," Dani said. "Go on so my husband can wash the dishes with me."

"Did I agree to wash the dishes?" Maverick teased, squinting one eye.

"I'll let you seduce me by the sink," she said, standing and grabbing two empty plates as she winked.

"Hot damn. Hand me a sponge, woman."

Dominic saluted them and thanked Dani for dinner before heading to find Arianna. Since he'd developed an insatiable need to know her whereabouts after his injury, he knew she liked to watch the sun set atop the old hill that crested behind the school where the withered pavement met the forest.

Exiting the double doors, he trailed over the asphalt and up the grass-covered hill, marveling at how tall and regal she appeared in the waning light of the sun. It washed over her bronzed skin, her shoulders and neck visible under her black tank top. He approached slowly, annoyance welling when her shoulders tensed.

"Can't get any damn privacy on this godforsaken compound," she muttered, staring in the distance as he neared, refusing to turn and acknowledge him.

The defiant gesture only made him more determined to infiltrate those thick walls. Stepping beside her, he slid his hands in his back pockets, gazing at the orange glow of the setting sun.

"We'll be more effective together," he finally said, judging her reaction from the corner of his eye as he stood firm. "And I'm fine with you being in charge."

She shot him a droll look. "Is that so? I wasn't aware I asked your permission."

Cocking a brow, he turned slightly toward her. "You haven't. Yet. There might be a time for that, but I don't think we're there yet."

Rotating to face him, she held up a finger. "This is about rescuing Raquel and making contact with Tristan. That's all. We'll work together as teammates and return to the compound once we've accomplished our task so we can formulate next steps. I don't know what nonsense Dani filled your head with, but I want no part of it."

Crossing his arms, he planted his feet as he waited. "Are you done?"

Scoffing, she turned away to stare at the horizon again, perhaps so he wouldn't see the emotion in those stunning eyes. "Yeah. And you're damn right I'm in charge." Grimacing, she began kneading the muscle between her neck and shoulder. "Damn it. I think I pulled something when I did weights today."

Sliding behind her—carefully, so she didn't run—he gently encircled her wrist. She bristled, her nostrils flaring as he slowly lowered her arm. Replacing her fingers with his, he began to massage her inflamed muscle.

Her throat bobbed as she continued to stare at the yellow-orange glow in the distance. The pulse on the free side of her neck throbbed in tandem with his firm movements, indicating she wasn't as unaffected by his touch as she portrayed.

Leaning closer, he could see the fine black hairs that were beginning to grow on the shaved side of her head. Placing his lips near the shell of her ear, he softly spoke. "You have a knot."

"No shit."

Breathing a laugh, he continued to work the muscle. She eventually closed her eyes and leaned her head forward, allowing him greater access. Joy reverberated in every cell of his skin as she opened herself to him, if only slightly.

"When we were in the lab—"

"I don't want to discuss that," she interrupted. "I told you—"

"When we were in the lab," he repeated, squeezing her shoulder as she grunted, "I was under the impression you didn't want me to die. Was I wrong about that?"

Sighing, she shook her head. "Of course I didn't want you to die." His fingers mourned the loss of her soft skin as she drew away and turned to face him. Gazing into his eyes, her tone was solemn. "But I'm a proud woman, Dom, and I'm not some fucking rom-com movie heroine."

His lips twitched. "No one would accuse you of that, Ari. Especially not me."

Mirth flashed across her strong features before they returned to the firm mask he was used to. "I'm not Dani. Get that through your fucking head. I don't need saving and I sure as hell don't need a man. We'll accomplish our mission and that's it. Are we clear?"

His eyes darted back and forth between hers as that palpable energy resonated between them. Deciding now wasn't the time to fight this battle, he relented. "We're clear."

"Good." With a nod, she breezed by him and began trudging down the hill.

"I just have one question," he called, hope surging in his chest when she halted.

"Yeah?"

"Who are you trying to convince? Me? Or yourself?"

Her features contorted into the scowl he'd somehow come to treasure before she lifted her hand and extended the middle finger. Unable to contain his grin, he absorbed her angry glare before she resumed the trek and disappeared into the school.

Facing the now-gray horizon, Dominic anticipated being near her as they completed their mission. Her goals were clear: rescue Raquel and acquire Tristan as an ally.

Dominic shared those goals, but he also had one more he was determined to accomplish: he was going to shatter Arianna's walls if it fucking killed him. And then, he was going to divest her of the notion she was in charge.

For, when he finally infiltrated her steely defenses, Dominic would revel in showing her how pleasurable taking orders from the *right* man could be...

Chapter 6

T he next morning, Arianna sat beside Dominic in the office of the abandoned gas station. After a restless night spent thinking about the upcoming mission, she felt a twinge of guilt that she'd stormed off after their conversation. Even if she wanted to go alone, he was intent on helping her, and there was honor in that. Plus, he'd agreed she should lead the mission, which deflated her need to argue with him—about *that* at least. Pity, since arguing with Dom was one of her favorite pastimes.

Perhaps her favorite of all, if she was being honest.

Once they were finished with Arthur's briefing, she promised to make peace with her unwanted companion. The decision had been made. She could at least try to be amenable. Even if the idea made her grit her teeth in frustration.

Shaking her head, she willed herself back to the mission at hand. Arthur sat on the edge of the desk as he rotated what appeared to be a homemade transmitter in his hands.

"This was fashioned by a self-proclaimed geek here on the compound," he said as he slowly showed off the device. "If one has a shortwave radio and knows the frequency, they can receive secret messages."

Lifting the nearby radio, he sat it on the edge of the desk and raised the antenna. Arianna vaguely remembered radio units from her childhood but wasn't intricately familiar with them.

"It's confusing after living with cell phones and internet for so long," Arthur said, smiling at her perplexed expression. "But it's all we've got left. You can leave this radio with Tristan and tell him to tune to the 4930 Khz frequency. I'll communicate with him in Morse code until I verify his identity. Then I'll create a new code between us to plan the siege on the city."

Arianna tilted her head in agreement. "Good idea. No one can intercept the messages if they don't know the code."

"Bingo." Arthur handed her the radio, and she slipped it into her backpack.

"Now, let's talk cars," Arianna said, a twinge of excitement in her voice. "I'm hoping you have a red 1964 Porche 911 with my name on it."

Arthur tossed back his head and laughed. "I'm not sure whether to deride your optimism or admire your taste in cars." Rising, he gestured for them to follow him outside. "Your choices are a bit less exciting. Blue sedan. Black pickup. White SUV," he finished, pointing at each car parked beside the building.

Arianna glanced at Dominic. "I think the sedan is best. It will get good gas mileage, and we can find a place outside the wall to hide it until we need to return."

Dominic rubbed his chin as his eyes narrowed. "The pickup and the SUV will give us more cover if we get attacked by any deserters or Sen Force troops on the journey."

"Yeah, but they'll guzzle more gas and are harder to hide in a forested area."

Dominic grinned at Arthur. "She's the boss. We'll take the sedan. You've calculated the optimal route?"

"It's best if you take old Route 7. It's more rural than other roads, so it will hopefully keep you off the radar." Reaching behind his back, he pulled a folded map from his belt. "I've marked the route for you. It will take you a little less than three hours to get to DC, and you'll end up near the old Chain Bridge Forest neighborhood, where you can hopefully find a good spot to hide the car. That neighborhood was abandoned when the residents moved inside the city walls."

"And then we'll cross the Potomac River and do our best to infiltrate the wall unnoticed," Arianna said, arching a brow as she took the map. "It's going to be fun."

Arthur smiled. "I like your sense of adventure, Arianna. As we've discussed, crossing the Chain Bridge is the best choice since it's the narrowest part of the river. My informants tell me there's a vulnerable spot in the wall about a mile south that's only patrolled by two Sen Force soldiers."

"Are there cameras as well?" Arianna asked.

"Yes. One on each side of the vulnerability. You'll need to shoot them to disarm them after you disable the guards. Since we're trying to save lives here instead of end them, I left some tranquilizing guns in the travel pack I prepared for you." He tapped his neck. "Shoot them here and the guards will be out for hours."

"We appreciate the supplies," Dominic said. "I'm assuming you'll give us real guns too?"

"The travel pack is full of cash, a few gold bars and two hand guns," he said, gesturing toward the office they'd just vacated. "I also left some bullets, but my supply is limited."

"Then we'll have to be precise," Dominic said. "We plan to leave around noon so we have time to stash the car and hike to the crossing once it gets dark. Our chances of breaching the wall are better under the cover of night."

"I wish you both a successful mission," Arthur said, extending his hand to shake Arianna's and then Dominic's. After giving them both a good-natured salute, he pivoted and headed toward the main path that led to the center of the compound.

"He's thorough. I'll give him that," Arianna said, gripping the straps of her backpack as she stared up at Dom. His six-foot-six height and broad shoulders made him one of the only men she'd ever found physically imposing. And yet, there was an innate gentleness under his stoic exterior. One that made her feel safe and slightly terrified at the same time. It was that gentleness that called to her when she closed her eyes late at night and imagined his deep voice in her ear as he ran his fingers over her skin...

"Who's going to drive?" she asked, observing his jagged scar glint in the sunlight. It was somehow ominous and sexy at the same time, and she wondered why it only served to increase her attraction to him. It made no sense, but she yearned to trace her finger over the ragged laceration. To trail from the edge of his dark eyebrow, over that firm nose, and to the corner of the full lips she'd envisioned kissing the most sensitive places of her body too many times to count.

"We can take shifts," he said, shrugging. "I'm sure you'll have to stop and pee every hour."

"*Pfft*," she said, unable to control her grin at his teasing. "I've got kidneys of steel. You'll see."

Dominic smiled before glancing at the car. "We need to stock up on water and food. Not too much but enough to sustain us if something goes wrong."

"I'll raid the kitchen at the school." Kicking the ground with the toe of her boot, she cleared her throat. "I...uh..."

"Yesssss?" he asked, arching a brow.

"Well, I just..." Huffing, she rolled her eyes. "I know I'm not the easiest person..."

"You? You're a basket of butterflies, Ari."

Expelling a breath, she stared into his deep brown eyes. "I guess you're going to use my nickname whether I like it or not."

He stepped closer, forcing her to tilt her head. Determined not to shrink, she straightened her spine.

Leaning forward, he spoke in that butter-rich tone as his warm breath washed over her cheeks. "Does it really bother you?"

Her throat bobbed as she contemplated. "It's something people who know me call me. And you don't know me."

He recoiled slightly, hurt flashing across his features before he shook his head. "I know enough. I know you were trying to thank me for coming with you just now, even if you did a piss poor job at it."

Scoffing, she rolled her eyes. "That's what I get for trying to be nice."

"And I know we're going to have the best outcome if we get along. So, let's both just admit we're in this together and be nice to each other."

"I'm nice," she said, frowning.

"Oh, yeah? I really enjoyed you flipping me the bird yesterday."

She bit her lip, loving the resulting flare in his eyes. The sizzling energy between them had only intensified since his injury, even if she refused to acknowledge it.

"I'll try to be nice," she said, capitulating. "It's not really my MO."

Leaning closer, he tilted his head as he studied her. "I think Chris and the other kids would beg to differ. And Dani and Mav too. You're nice in your own way. Just not to me. I wonder why?"

"Because you're annoying," she snapped before quickly realizing it was that knee-jerk reaction she needed to control. "We both annoy the hell out of each other. But I don't want to argue with you. We need to be in sync. So I'll do better."

"You don't annoy me," he said, his tone genuine. "Not anymore. Getting shot will open a man's eyes."

"I've heard you tell Mav you want to strangle me."

"Maybe once or twice," he said, grinning. "But I think you're a good person under that harsh exterior, and it's time for us to be friends."

"Friends," she responded morosely.

"For now." His eyes lowered to her neck and collarbone before lifting back to hers. A challenge simmered deep in the brown orbs, and her knees threatened to buckle. "I'm game if you are."

Overwhelmed with the intensity between them, she took a step back. "Okay, *friend*. We'll give that a try. Maybe you can..." She trailed off, suddenly embarrassed for some reason.

Dark eyebrows lifted as he waited.

"I mean...uh, maybe you can tell me about Pam and your parents. I've always wanted to hear the story from you, and I can probably relate since my mom and my birth parents…you know…" Fumbling, she shook her head. "Shit, I'm bad at this."

His warm laughter surrounded her as he reassuringly cupped her upper arm, causing tiny bumps to spring up underneath his palm. "You're doing fine. And I'd love to tell you about them. You've never asked so I didn't want to bother you with my sad stories."

"I stopped asking people to share their stories with me a long time ago" was her solemn response. "And you always had Dani to talk to." He opened his mouth to respond, and she held up a hand. "Regardless, I'm asking now. In the whole spirit of being *friends*." She made quotation marks with her fingers.

Something akin to admiration laced his features. "I know it wasn't easy for you to ask. Someday, maybe you'll tell me why you stay locked inside that shell." He gently tapped her shoulder above her collarbone. "I think you've got some stories to tell too."

Arianna didn't share her pain with anyone. No matter how friendly they became, she couldn't fathom opening herself up to Dominic and exposing the deep-rooted ache she'd always felt just by being *her*. She was an outsider. Different. She always had been since she'd lost every blood relative at four years old.

Cynthia Lawson had brought her into their family, and Arianna had loved her to distraction, but she'd never shaken the feeling of not belonging. Instead of trying to fit in, she'd eventually accepted her place in the world and reacted accordingly. Even her hair was a fuck-you to the norm.

That lack of belonging was where her deep-rooted need to have a biological child stemmed from. Arianna longed to have at least one person on the planet who shared her blood. Who was *part* of her. Someone who wouldn't be able to hurt or leave her as so many others had.

A child she could love without fear.

To protect that child, she would create a safe space. A place only for the two of them, secluded and serene. A place where her child felt wholly loved and connected to the mother who'd born her.

Arianna craved that connection in ways that almost frightened her sometimes. But she guessed that meant she hadn't completely given up on feeling basic human emotion, so she allowed the need to exist deep in her heart.

"Oh, yeah," Dominic said, his smile deepening. "There's a lot to unleash in there. I'd love to hear it. Even strong people need a shoulder to lean on sometimes."

"Let's start with your stories and we'll get to mine eventually," she said, inwardly promising she'd never share her most personal stories with him. But she was a damn good listener, and she'd always imagined comforting him like Dani had. Did she have the capacity to do it? That remained to be seen. But at least she could try. "But don't piss me off or we'll be back to square one."

Laughter bellowed from his throat as he shook his head. "Damn, you're funny. Do people know you're this funny?"

"People don't know me at all. That was kind of my point."

His expression turned reverent as he gazed at her. "Well, I can't wait to be one of the few that do."

Her mouth turned dry as she licked the roof, her heartbeat quickening as she looked into his eyes. Struggling to breathe, she tried to form a pithy comeback, but it lodged in her throat.

"You don't have to end every conversation with a retort, Arianna," he said, smiling as his eyes slowly darted between hers. "Come on. Let's check the tires on the sedan and make sure it's ready."

With that, the man who consumed her every thought walked toward the car, seemingly oblivious that her body was on fire and ready to explode. As he crouched down beside the tire to examine the ridges, one striking thought blazed through her mind: *Girl, you're in trouble.*

Pushing it aside, she trailed over to help her *friend* prepare for their journey.

Chapter 7

T he sedan was prepped and ready to go promptly at noon. Maverick hugged Arianna before Dani stepped in to crush her in a deep embrace.

"Pretty strong grip for a scientist," Arianna teased, squeezing her back. "Get that antidote done while we're gone, okay?"

Dani released her and saluted. "Ten-four. Be safe, Ari. I love you."

"Love you too," Arianna softly replied as Chris scampered toward her, a trinket in his small hand.

"My sister made this for you," he said, holding up what looked to be a charm bracelet. "I told her bracelets were dumb, but this one is pretty cool."

Arianna's heart swelled as she examined it. A tiny leather strap held various acorns and dried flowers, and it was quite pretty.

"Tell Jenny I said thanks," she said, sliding it onto her wrist. "And thank you too. Be good while I'm gone, okay, kid?"

Chris nodded, his hair flying in the light breeze before he turned and jogged away. Arianna glanced toward Dominic, noticing the admiration in his expression. Rolling her eyes, she straightened her shoulders, not wanting to come off as a damn sap. "Let's go. I'll drive first shift."

They said their last goodbyes and hopped into the sedan. Dominic's large body barely folded into the car, and he adjusted the seat to accommodate his long legs. Chris and several other kids appeared beside the car, running along as she slowly drove toward the entrance. They eventually disappeared from view as she gained speed before stopping at the large doors that comprised the entrance to the compound.

Arthur Reyes stood guard, surrounded by several armed men. He lifted his hand and circled it, and two of the men pushed each massive door open. Waving to them, Arianna put the car in drive and headed outside of the walls for the first time in several weeks.

As they pulled onto the rural roads, Arianna took in the signs of desolation and destruction. Power lines lay strewn across fields, disconnected and disassembled for survivors to use for warmth and kindling. Several houses they passed had large red Xs on the front doors—the symbol that the residents had died when society collapsed. Most of the businesses were looted, their windows broken as dirty signs hung above empty stores.

Millions had died over the past few years. Most from EverLife addiction. Some from collateral damage from the fact that Luthor Cromwell had ordered the Sen Force troops to destroy all electricity and technology outside the Ten Cities. Only those cities—DC, Miami, New York and the other largest cities in America—had been spared. Cromwell now controlled what was left of the US Army, and his newly renamed Sen Force troops had pledged their loyalty. That was the cost of protecting their families inside the walls, where technology and societal norms still existed in some capacity.

"You look serious over there," Dominic said, lifting his eyebrows.

"I was thinking about our former counterparts. All the soldiers who pledged their allegiance to Cromwell so easily. It's going to be tough to mount an offensive if they remain loyal to him."

"Lack of a strong leader will forge weak alliances," Dominic said. "We need someone to fill the void and give them a reason to fight for good instead of evil."

"And you think Reyes is that man?"

Lifting a shoulder, he shrugged. "I think he's a big step up from Cromwell. And he wants the job, which makes him just crazy enough to possibly succeed."

Arianna laughed. "For real. I'm done with war—and with people in general, if I'm being honest. Once we save the world, I'm going off the grid."

"Yeah?" Leaning his temple on the headrest, he studied her. "Where to?"

"None of your business. That's the entire point of disappearing. No one knows your destination."

His low-toned "hmm" caused her to give him the side eye.

"Did you have a comment?" she asked, her tone dripping with sarcasm.

"Nope," he said, spreading the map Arthur had given them over his lap. "I'm just really good at finding people who don't want to be found. I did it with terrorists in Pakistan and Afghanistan for years."

"Dani and Mav will be settled down with kids by then, so finding me is irrelevant. I'll visit them when I want to see them."

He just uttered another grunt, causing her to squish her fingers on the wheel, imagining it was his throat. It's not like he would come looking for her. Sure, they were teammates because circumstances demanded it, but once they weren't forced together, she doubted he'd care to look for her. Dominic had his own life, after all.

The subject of her thoughts studied the map as she drove, and she assumed the conversation was finished until he spoke.

"You don't want to have kids? The way you are with Chris and the others... You'd be great, Ari."

"I know," she said, trying to remain nonchalant at the reverence in his voice. "I'll just be great without a partner."

A slow smile curled across those full lips. "Yeah, but wouldn't it be more fun to do it with someone else?"

She exhaled an annoyed breath. "Never met anyone I want to spend that much time with. I'm all set."

He shot her a disbelieving glance but remained silent. Reminding herself not to tangle with him since she'd promised to be nice, she pressed her lips together, determined to end the uncomfortable conversation.

"Just continue on this road for forty-five minutes and then we'll hit the fork that leads to Route 127. That eventually merges with Route 7."

Arianna clenched her jaw. "Got it."

His lips twitched as he glanced toward her. "I know you studied the map and want to tell me to fuck off. I appreciate your restraint."

Breathing a laugh, she relaxed her shoulders. It was amazing how well he could read her. And somewhat terrifying too. "I know you're trying to help." She pushed the power button on the radio and selected the CD option. "Whoever owned this car was a huge Grateful Dead fan. Get ready to binge some Jerry Garcia."

"I like the Dead," he said, stretching out his legs and resting his hands behind his head. "Bring it on."

They drove as Jerry serenaded them, the silence between them easy. Arianna wasn't really a talker and liked the fact they could chill without it being weird.

When they reached the juncture with Route 127, she pulled the car into a wooded area and parked.

"You didn't even make it an hour," he teased, the curve of his lips sexy as he reached for the handle.

"I had an extra cup of coffee for the drive," she retorted, exiting the car and stretching. "Give me a break." Observing the trees, she pointed to one. "I'm going to take care of business over there. Then I'll keep watch while you go."

Dominic nodded, doing his own stretches as she observed the white bandage on his neck. It moved as he rotated and swung his arms, and she swallowed thickly, thankful he'd accompanied her even if he wasn't fully recovered.

"If you're not going to go, I'll go—"

"Yeah, sorry," she said, shaking her head before approaching the tree. After surveying the area, she relieved herself before heading back and ushering Dominic into the woods.

He returned, his hands still fastening his belt buckle, and she felt a rush of heat over every inch of her skin. Had he ever used that belt to restrain a lover? And why was the thought so damn hot?

Although Arianna was tough as nails, she'd always fantasized about having a dominant lover. Someone who could handle her rigid demeanor and urge her to let go. To actually *feel* like the woman the world rarely allowed her to be...

The belt clicked simultaneously as her gaze rose to lock with his. Those brown eyes simmered as he hooked his thumbs in the belt, his eyes raking over her as she struggled to breathe.

"You ready?" he asked in that deep baritone that made her bones liquify.

"Uh, yeah. You want to drive the next leg?"

"Sure."

He maneuvered his large body into the car, adjusting the seat farther back as she sat beside him. Thick, tattooed arms turned the wheel as they resumed the drive, and Arianna noted the broken pavement on the two-lane road as she stared out the window.

Something glinted in the side mirror and she leaned forward, squinting at the reflection. As her heartbeat quickened, she turned to look through the back window.

"What is it?" Dominic asked, his eyes drifting toward the rearview mirror.

"I thought I saw something." The road stretched behind them, clear and desolate.

"Hard for stragglers to find gas unless they got it from a compound," he said, the words reassuring although his shoulders were tense.

Nodding, she maneuvered back into the seat and ran a hand over the fuzz now growing over the bald side of her head. "I'll keep an eye out. Just drive and keep up the pace. My grandpa drives faster than you."

"I'm assuming your grandpa is dead," he said, arching a sardonic brow. "May he rest in peace."

"And he still drives faster than you. Kick it into gear, old man."

Arianna knew Dominic was in his early forties, so they were close in age since her fortieth birthday was fast approaching. Still, it was fun to chide him—and he definitely drove at a slower pace than the one she'd set earlier.

When they reached the juncture of Route 127 and Route 7, they stopped to take another break in a wooded area. Dominic headed into the brush first, followed quickly by Arianna, who admitted she needed more bathroom breaks than she had in her twenties. But she'd never admit that Dominic was right—to his face, at least.

She'd barely gotten her pants zipped when she heard a twig snap behind her. Gasping, she pulled the gun from her belt and aimed at the origin of the sounds. Ears perked, she waited, keeping her breathing calm so it didn't obstruct her hearing.

Another twig snapped and she whirled, grip firm on the gun as she planted her feet. A man stepped out from behind the brush, gun held firm as he grinned. "Well, well. What do we have here?"

Arianna felt a presence behind her and rotated—fast as lightning—and jutted the base of her hand into a man's throat. The karate chop caused the man to gasp before he gripped his neck. Aiming the gun, she shot his kneecap.

The man screamed with pain before dropping to the ground and gripping his knee. Turning back, she aimed between the other man's eyes. "I won't aim for your knee," she said through clenched teeth. "So you can run or you can die. Your choice."

Fear flashed in his eyes as he spoke into the watch around his wrist. "They're approaching on Route 7—"

The man's eyes widened before a trickle of blood appeared between his eyes. The red liquid glimmered in the afternoon sun as it ran toward his nose before he collapsed on the ground.

"Good shot," she said, sensing Dominic beside her. "I was going to let him live...I think. The bastard didn't even let me get my pants buttoned. Asshole." She placed the gun in the holster at her waist, annoyed that her hands were slightly shaking. She was usually steady on her feet, but being attacked while finishing up taking a piss would make anyone feel vulnerable.

"Here," Dominic said, closing in and covering her hands. "Just breathe." Deft fingers encircled the button, lacing it through the hole as she expelled a calming breath. Once fastened, he rested his palm over her hip, the gesture comforting as he gauged her reaction. "Sorry I wasn't there. I'd opened the trunk to get some water—"

"It's fine," she said, her voice raspy as she backed away from his stabilizing hand at her waist, surprised how much she wanted to lean toward him and let him support her. Arianna never leaned on *anyone*, and the uncomfortable feelings that surfaced were sticky and raw.

Glancing over, she noticed Mr. No More Kneecap was unconscious. "What are we going to do with him?"

"We're going to wake him up and ask him who that was on the other end of his watch," Dominic said, pointing to the dead attacker. "They're not wearing Sen Force uniforms, but they don't have deserter marks either. They could be independent mercenaries."

Mr. No More Kneecap groaned, his eyes fluttering as he lolled on the ground. "I'm not telling you shit," he rasped.

Arianna observed him clutch the gun at his side, and she lurched but was too late. The man lifted the gun to his temple and released a clean shot.

"No!" she yelled, drawn back by Dominic's firm grip around her arm. "Damn it, I wanted to question him."

The man released his last breath, his body going limp on the ground as she sighed. "Let's take both watches as evidence. Maybe we can figure out who they were communicating with."

"They might have trackers," Dominic said, striding over to remove the far man's watch.

"He already told whoever was on the other end we were approaching on Route 7. Tracker or not, they know we're coming." Leaning down, she removed the other watch.

Returning to Dominic's side, she lifted the gadget, studying it. "Looks like a modified smart watch. Maybe it has radio technology like Reyes is using."

"Maybe. Come on. I don't want to linger here any longer."

Arianna followed him back to the car, unsettled at the fact that someone knew they were approaching DC. Wondering who the hell was on the other end of the transmission, she climbed into the car, quiet and pensive as they resumed their trek.

Chapter 8

They arrived at the abandoned Chain Bridge Forest neighborhood as the sun hung low in the afternoon sky. Dominic spotted an overgrown path and followed it until the car was shrouded by trees.

"It's as good a spot as any," Arianna said, stretching before she reached in the back seat and began securing her supplies.

"Hopefully it will be here when we get back."

After shrugging on her backpack—filled with ammunition, small rations of food, and the money Reyes had given them—she jerked her head. "Let's go."

They hiked quietly through the forest, both alert as they listened for signs of life. Aside from the random squirrels and birds, all was clear.

Dominic's hand encircled hers, drawing her to a stop as she frowned. "The crossing is that way."

"I know," he said, squeezing her fingers. "But look at that."

Arianna followed his gaze, her eyes widening at the words spray-painted on the tree: *Cromwell must die.*

"A sign of the rebellion Reyes mentioned," she said.

Leaning closer, he studied the writing. "Could be deserters, but the message is pretty clear."

"Looks like Tristan might get his war after all."

Dominic nodded before resuming the hike, and Arianna followed him, thoughtful as they meandered through the forest.

As the sky turned from cloud-spattered blue to early evening orange, the trees cleared and they approached the riverbank. Arianna's black boots pushed into the soft ground as she gazed across the gurgling water.

"Arthur said it will come up to our waist if we cross here." Clutching the straps of her pack, she sighed. "Might as well get on with it. We'll need to dry off on the other side so we don't leave a trail of mud."

"I'll lead—"

"I thought we agreed I was the leader of this mission," she interrupted.

"You are, but my mom raised me to be a gentleman." Stepping forward, he planted a foot in the water and turned back, extending his hand.

Arianna did her best to ignore the flip-flop of the organ now pounding in her chest as she slipped her hand in his.

He led her down, air hissing through her teeth as the cold water rushed against her legs through her black pants. "I thought it would be warmer."

"It's almost fall," he said, releasing her hand to wade through the water a few feet in front of her. "Must be getting some colder flow from the north."

Arianna grunted as she followed him, aware of the tiny chill bumps that lifted the hairs on her arms. The water breached her waist, and she breathed a sigh of relief they were halfway through. She scanned the tall metal wall that glowed in the last waning sunlight, wondering if they were being watched. She rested her palm on the handle of the gun at her waist, comforted by the fact she could at least put up a good fight if they were ambushed.

Dusk had settled in by the time they crested the other side. Dominic led her to a large tree before removing the towel from his pack. He dried his legs and boots before touching the bandage at his neck. Grimacing, he pulled it off and gently rubbed the tender skin.

"Does it hurt?" she asked, feeling slightly guilty that she'd been such an ass about him coming on the trip when he was still recovering.

"More like a throbbing itch," he said, shaking his head. "I want to scratch it so fucking badly."

"Here." Taking his towel, she located a dry spot and tenderly dabbed his wound. "I'm in awe of how fast you're healing. And I..." Drifting off, she was flooded of visions of him bleeding profusely on the squalid Sendaxa lab floor. "I'm really glad you're okay, Dom."

"I know you are." His velvet voice washed over her, smooth as melted butter slipping into every cranny of a warm English muffin.

Swallowing thickly, she backed away and dried her pants before shaking out the towel. Folding it, she handed it to him so he could stuff it back in his pack.

"Remain alert," he softly commanded. "I'm going first. But you're still the boss."

"Dom—"

"I'm going first," he repeated, his tone unequivocal. "Let's go."

Narrowing her eyes, she nodded and pulled her gun from her holster. They walked slowly toward the wall, the metal slabs growing taller and more menacing as they approached. When they reached the perimeter, she peered toward the top, which she estimated to be thirty feet high.

"No lookouts or cameras spotted, but that doesn't mean they aren't there."

"Agreed" was Domnic's soft reply. "Arthur said the weak spot in the wall was about a mile south."

They trailed along the wall, Arianna following close behind Dominic, unwilling to examine why she felt so comfortable letting him lead. She seldom trusted people enough to give them that much control, but he was a rare exception. Somewhere along the way, she'd come to trust him more than anyone except Dani and Maverick. Grappling with the weight of the realization, she rapidly shook her head, reminding herself to focus on the task at hand.

Arianna could feel the heat from his large frame as she stayed close behind him. Dusk turned to darkness, and he pulled out a small flashlight, illuminating the juncture where the wall met the grass. Ariana mentally calculated the distance and eventually tapped Dominic's shoulder.

"We've gone about a mile," she said, stopping to peruse the wall. "Let's start looking for the weak spot."

The sound of a gun cocking behind them caused Arianna's eyes to widen. Whirling around, she aimed into the darkness.

A man stepped forward, his strong features laced with annoyance and derision. "I've got several men within shooting distance. Lower the gun, Arianna."

Frustrated they'd been discovered, she sighed and followed Tristan Holder's command.

CHAPTER 9

D ominic placed his palm on Arianna's shoulder blade, silently reassuring her as he stared into Tristan's hazel eyes. They glinted in the darkness as the man slowly approached. He made a *tsk, tsk, tsk* sound before arching an eyebrow.

"Looks like someone's trying to break into the city."

"It was you on the other end of the transmission," Arianna said, her muscles tense under Dominic's hand.

Lifting his wrist, he rotated it in the dimness. "Smart watches still work in the city...*sometimes*. Hell of a thing. Cromwell allows some of us to use technology...for now."

"You already proved in the lab that you're not going to kill us," Dominic said. "So what's the next move?"

Tristan scrunched his features. "Killing you would be fun, but you're right. You're both more useful alive to me than dead. Speaking of, did you kill the spies who told me you were coming?"

"Yes." Arianna lifter her chin. "We didn't want to, but they attacked us. We killed one and the other took himself out."

"Pity." Craning his neck, he spoke to Dominic. "You have a bad habit of killing my men."

"Your men have a bad habit of making poor decisions."

Pursing his lips, Tristan nodded. "Can't argue with that. Well, now that we're all here, let's get the party started. I need you two to do something for me. Once you complete the task, I'll tell you where Raquel is." His gaze traveled to Arianna. "I assume that's why you're here."

"We're not doing any *task* for you," she said, bristling. "We're here to get my sister, do some reconnaissance, and give you a message from Arthur Reyes. After that, we're out."

A slightly sinister chuckle left Tristan's chest. "So combative. The Lawson sisters have that in common."

Concern laced Arianna's features. "Is Raquel okay? I swear, if you or Cromwell have hurt her—"

"She's fine," he said, showing his palm. "I've been protecting her."

Arianna crossed her arms and expelled a dismissive breath. "I bet."

"Luthor has tasked her with amplifying both EverLife and the pure antidote. He wants the former to be stronger and the latter to be weaker but still effective. I'm no scientist, but she seems to be making progress."

"To what end?" Dominic asked.

Tristan shrugged. "Addicts are easy to control. The more effective the drug, the more powerful he is. He speaks about raiding Arthur's compound to extradite Danica for public trial, but he hasn't acted on it yet."

"Why?" Arianna asked, rubbing her arm in the wake of the chilly air that swirled around the wall.

"Because he's developing a new drug. One similar to EverLife, although it doesn't extend lifespan. It increases muscle density and strength. Once it's ready, he's going to pump the Sen Force soldiers full of it and begin attacking the compounds. Arthur's compound will be first."

"Shit," Arianna breathed. "A real-life Captain America drug. Cromwell will be invincible with an army like that."

"Since we can't let that happen, I'm going to need you two to destroy the lab where that drug is being developed."

"Why can't you do it?"

"Because I can't be caught on camera working against Cromwell." Leaning forward, he flashed a sinister grin. "But *you* can."

"We don't have time for this—"

"If you want my alliance and you want me to lead you to Raquel, this is my price," Tristan interjected. "I assume Reyes wants someone on the inside to help his cause. I'm hoping he's going to start the war I so desperately want."

"It would be nice to dethrone Cromwell without war," Dominic muttered.

"That's a fantasy you should let go of now. There will be a war, and at the end of it, we'll see who rises from the ashes. I don't really care who takes over for Cromwell as long as I kill the bastard."

"And if we don't destroy the lab?" Arianna asked.

"I'll kill Raquel."

Scoffing, she turned to look at Dominic. "Maybe we should just shoot this motherfucker. He's really pissing me off."

"We need him, and he knows it," Dominic replied, warily eyeing Tristan. "You'll get us the explosives?"

"There's a hotel in LeDroit Park at the corner of 2nd and T Street where you can stay while you're here. It's off the grid and not very safe, but I think you two can handle yourselves." He smirked, causing Arianna to grit her teeth. "Devon at the front desk is expecting you. He likes to be paid in gold. I'm assuming Reyes provided that, along with cash."

Arianna gave a curt nod.

"He'll put you up in a room for a few days so you can get the job done. I left a bag with him that has a map of the lab and all the materials you'll need. It has a lock with the code 10-09."

"Raquel's birthday," Arianna said softly. Sighing, she rubbed her forehead. "If we agree to do this, I'm going to need assurance Raquel is okay. I still have contacts here and have no doubt I can track your location in a matter of hours."

"There's no need to come looking for me, Arianna. I want information and action as much as you. And if you're looking for intel on a rebellion, I'm happy to tell you what I know."

"We assumed you'd be part of the rebellion," Dominic said.

"I want to murder Luther and that's my primary goal. Others have the goal of taking him down and trying to rebuild society. I don't know who all the players are yet. I think my proximity to Luthor keeps the rebellion leaders from approaching me." Lifting a finger, he arched a brow. "Remember, I technically work for Luthor. I have reasons I need to keep him close and keep up that deception. Whoever is leading the rebellion doesn't trust me yet."

"That makes two of us," Arianna muttered.

"Taking out Dr. Ziegler's lab is important for the future of any rebellion," he continued. "You must understand that Cromwell can't get his hands on a super-soldier drug. It would cement his future as leader for decades."

Dominic looked at Arianna, seeing the same acknowledgment in her expression that welled in his gut.

"And we're just supposed to believe this isn't a trap for us to walk into? Since you do technically work for Cromwell," she said, repeating his words.

Sighing, Tristan rolled his eyes. "So dramatic. I want the super-soldier drug destroyed and have no one inside the wall I trust to do it. You two are pretty effective at blowing shit up," he said, pointing between them. "So why not help me? It's a small price to pay for my help in return."

Inhaling a labored breath, Arianna nodded. "Fine. It will save us from having to find our own lodging, which would waste valuable time. I'm in if you are," she said to Dominic.

He nodded, and Arianna turned back to Tristan. "We'll surveil the lab and get the job done as quickly as possible. After that, how will we know where to find you?"

"I'll find you," he said, backing away. "And don't get caught. You're on Cromwell's turf now, and he'll most likely publicly execute you two if he gets his hands on you. When you're finished, I'll lead you to Raquel, although I'm not sure she'll go with you. She's feistier than I originally thought."

"She'll come with us even if I have to drag her out of this fucking city," Arianna said.

Tristan pointed toward the wall. "Wait ten minutes and then enter a hundred yards south of here. Two soldiers guard that section of the wall, but I'm sure Reyes already armed you with that information. Once you take them out, there's a rip in the metal where you can ease through. You'll have to feel around to find it. There are two cameras atop the wall that one of my cyber-tech soldiers rewired so the feed is on a loop."

"Crafty," Dominic said, impressed with his forethought.

"There shouldn't be any soldiers on the other side, but definitely stay inconspicuous. It will take you a few hours to walk to LeDroit Park, and Devon knows you're coming."

With one last nod, he breezed past them, heading toward the nearby woods.

"You're not going back inside the city?" she asked.

"I have something to attend to outside the walls," he said cryptically. "I'll be keeping an eye on you both. Be careful."

"Wait," Arianna said, removing her pack and digging out the radio. "Arthur wants to communicate with you using Morse code and on the 4930 Khz radio frequency. He wants to see if you're amenable to working together."

"I might be," Tristan said, taking the radio, "if he agrees to start the war I'm looking for. I've noted the frequency," he tapped his temple. "Thank you. Work fast and good luck." Pivoting, he advanced toward the nearby woods, disappearing between the trees under the starlit sky.

"Bossy fucking bastard," Arianna said, lifting hesitant eyes to Dominic's. "Are we really going to do this?"

"Honestly? It gives us a place to stay and a reason to stay in contact with Tristan, who claims to know Raquel's whereabouts. Plus, blowing shit up with you will be fun."

Her breathy laugh washed over his skin, and he reveled in her proximity. Long, dark eyelashes glistened in the moonlight as she stared at him, contemplating.

"Well, then I guess we need to haul ass to LeDroit Park. From what I remember, it's about seven miles from here. I wouldn't mind a bed and a roof over our heads so I can sleep."

Nodding, he loaded the tranquilizer guns and handed one to her. "We only have four darts, but I'd rather not have to reload. Let's get a clean hit the first time."

"Done," Arianna said, gripping the gun.

They stalked slowly toward the vulnerability in the wall, ears perked as they listened for danger. When they were twenty yards away, Dominic spotted two guards slowly pacing around the wall.

"You take the one on the left and I'll get the one on the right."

With a tilt of her head, she moved forward in the darkness, extending the gun and squinting one eye as she aimed.

Watching Arianna wield a weapon was a thing of beauty. Entranced by her, he reminded himself to stay focused. Her jaw clenched seconds before a puff sounded from the barrel of the gun. The soldier on the other end gasped, clutching his neck as the dart connected.

The second soldier whirled to face his counterpart, and Dominic seized the situation. Aiming at the man's exposed jugular, he released the dart, adrenaline surging through his veins when it met its mark. Both men grasped their necks before falling to the ground, unconscious.

They approached the fallen men cautiously, Arianna gently kicking one in his thigh to make sure he was down. Crouching, she removed the rifle from his shoulder. "Don't mind if I do. This will pair nicely with my Glock. Thanks, buddy."

Dominic quickly divested the other soldier of his rifle and slung it over his shoulder. Arianna approached the grooved metal wall and ran her hands over it. Her eyes grew wide when she felt a break in the consistency and stuck her hand through. "Here it is. Help me pull it back."

Dominic tugged the metal, opening a small hole for her to crawl through. After he squeezed his large frame through, they reset the metallic flap. Arianna wiped her hands on her pants as she stared at the glow of the far-off city. "It's been a while since I've seen lights that bright."

"I miss the city sometimes, but I doubt it's anything like what I remember. This place is a gilded cage for addicts," he said. Pointing toward the lights, he squinted. "Let's walk along the river until we hit K Street. Then we'll veer east."

Nodding, Arianna walked beside him in comfortable silence. Talking would've made noise, and they needed to remain alert. Eventually, they reached K Street and veered toward LeDroit Park.

Although the city twinkled in the distance, Dominic noticed the signs of their post-apocalyptic world. Many buildings had wooden boards nailed across the entrance, some with a red or black X spray-painted across them. As they walked along the paved but somewhat unkempt streets, they passed several families living in tents.

There were no cars on the roads, which created an eerie silence as the streetlights buzzed above, powered by energy from the remaining power plant to the city. Reyes had informed them that Cromwell directed most of the energy to the downtown region of the city he and the other wealthy cronies inhabited, leaving the rest of the city to function on generators or without energy at all.

Gas was now a high commodity since all trade from oil-producing nations had stopped. Each nation was now isolated with billions across the world dead. Bicycles and walking were the main modes of transport in the city, and Dominic doubted they'd even see a car until they approached downtown. Even then, they likely wouldn't see many.

Still, the city fared better than the black-market compounds, which had no access to resources they couldn't generate on their own.

Arianna frowned at the destruction as they paced. "So many homeless people," she said as they passed several more tents. "You'd think Cromwell would want to clean this up."

"It's a reminder for people inside the walls of what can happen if they don't stay compliant," Dominic said. "I doubt these people are getting any sort of clean antidote. He probably feeds them one that barely keeps them alive between EverLife injections."

"So fucking sad," she murmured, clutching the straps of her pack as they walked.

Some streets showed more destruction than others, and he observed clean, tree-lined streets in between the more run-down areas. Dominic figured these were the parts where the middle-class lived. Perhaps people who hadn't succumbed to EverLife addiction who still worked downtown and tried to live a normal life—or whatever amounted to "normal" in their desolate world.

After several hours of walking with only a few breaks, they entered the LeDroit Park section of the city.

"Damn, that was a long walk," Arianna said, rubbing her neck as they approached the corner of 2nd and T Streets. "I'm ready to crash."

Gazing up at the sign that read Mayflower Motel, Dominic raised his eyebrows. "This must be it."

The worn brick three-story building had seen better days, but if it had a bed and some running water, he'd be happy. The wooden door creaked as he pulled it open, gesturing Arianna inside before approaching the dimly lit front desk.

A man snored behind the desk, arms crossed across his chest as he leaned back in the black office chair. His feet rested on the counter before him, and Dominic cleared his throat.

The clerk's eyes flew open before he reached for the gun on the counter. Snaking his arm out, Dominic caught the man's wrist before he could grab the weapon.

"Calm down, man. Tristan sent us."

Recognition lit the clerk's eyes as he straightened his spine and gave them both a once-over. "Ah, the two rebels. He said you'd have gold for me." Leaning forward, he whispered, "If you also have a stash of EverLife, I take that as payment too."

Dominic scowled as he reached into the pack Arthur had prepared. "Just gold, man. I'm assuming you're Devon?"

"One and the same," he said, taking the gold bar. "This will get you a few days. After that, I'll need another bar."

"Fine," Arianna said with a nod. "Will that cover two rooms?"

Devon's lips curled into a mischievous smile as he glanced between them. "No pleasure on this business trip, hmmm?"

Reaching over the counter, Arianna clutched his collar as he yelped. "None of your fucking business. This is an important mission and we don't have time for small talk. Do you have two rooms?"

Sputtering, Devon shook his head as Arianna released his collar. "Only one," he rasped. "Sorry. I told Tristan we only had one vacancy. It has a double bed and a couch in the main room."

"That will do," Dominic said, his tone firm so Arianna wouldn't argue. "Give us the key and we'll let you get back to sleep. And if anyone asks about us, keep your mouth shut. Here's something for your silence." Drawing out several hundred-dollar bills, he set them on the counter. "If we finish our stay and you've remained silent, we'll give you another gold bar."

"What stay?" Devon asked cheekily, shrugging.

"Exactly," Arianna said, grabbing the key and the bag Devon set on the counter.

"That's from Tristan. It has improvised explosives inside, so be careful."

Arianna peered inside the bag before closing it. "I assume this dump doesn't have an elevator?"

"Your room is on the second floor, and no, you'll have to take the stairs." He pointed down a dim hallway. "You'll see them."

"Thanks, man," Dominic said with a salute. Arianna shot Devon one last stern glare before stalking away. Dominic followed her, his eyes focusing on her firm ass as she climbed.

He followed her to room 203, waving his hand in front of his nose when they stepped inside. "Smells musty."

"As long as it's relatively clean, who cares?" She opened the door in the small foyer and grinned. "Bingo. There are clean sheets and blankets in here. I'll sleep on the couch."

"No way," he said, reaching past her to grab a blanket. "I'll take the couch. You take the bed."

Her expression turned droll. "Dominic, you're still healing. I'm not that big of an asshole to deny you the bed. You need rest more than I do."

Without thinking, he gently encircled her wrist. Her pulse beat strongly beneath his fingers as he gazed into her eyes, mesmerized by the green and brown hues in their depths. "If you think I'd let you sleep on the couch, you know nothing about me. I'm old school, Ari, and you're taking the bed."

Her throat bobbed as she stared up at him, and the debate whether to argue with him flared across her strong features.

"You use the bathroom first and then I will. Hopefully there's hot water, but I'm not holding my breath."

"I'd argue with you," she whispered, gently tugging her wrist from his grasp, "but I'm honestly too damn tired to summon the energy."

Feeling the corner of his lips tick up, he gestured with his head. "Go on so I can get in there."

She hesitated for a few seconds before nodding and walking to the small table on the far side of the room. After setting Tristan's bag on top, she entered the bathroom that sat between the tiny main room and the bedroom. As she brushed her teeth and washed off the grime of the day, Dominic placed fresh sheets on the double bed. Their accommodations wouldn't be featured on a luxury homes tour, but the room was passable.

Arianna skirted by him, heading into the bedroom and closing the door so only a crack remained. Dominic entered the bathroom and washed his face and neck before brushing his teeth with the contents of the small travel case he'd packed. He examined his wound in the murky mirror, noting the most recent scab was peeling and the skin underneath appeared red and healthy. Pausing to express a moment of silent gratitude, he exited the bathroom to find Arianna making up the couch.

She spread a blanket atop the sheet she'd laid out under a pillow she retrieved from the closet. Straightening, she lifted a shoulder. "It's going to be uncomfortable. Are you sure?"

He nodded, inwardly acknowledging he wanted to sleep in the bed...with *her*. To wrap his body around every inch of her firm curves and rest his face in her nape as she slept. For a man who'd sworn off affection for so long, it was a strange sensation—but it was real. As real as the emotion on her stunning face had been when she'd gazed into his eyes and begged him not to die...

"Dom?"

"Yeah, I'm fine with uncomfortable. I slept on the ground in the Middle East for years." Approaching the couch, he tugged off his shirt before sitting down and removing his boots.

Arianna's eyes widened slightly as she backed away. Clearing her throat, she uttered a scratchy "Good night" before heading toward the bedroom.

"Ari?" he called from the couch.

Turning, she rested her hand on the doorframe, her body silhouetted by the faint lights that shone through the bedroom window. "Yeah?"

"Thanks for making up the couch. It's a nice gesture from a woman who tries so hard to pretend she doesn't care."

Her eyes narrowed as anger reddened her cheeks. Shooting him a glare, she stepped across the threshold and shut the door with a firm *thunk*.

Chuckling, Dominic lay back on the couch, resting his hands behind his head as he stared at the popcorn ceiling. Damn, he loved riling her. Shuffling under the blanket, he flipped to his side and clicked off the lamp on the side table.

Settling into the lumpy cushions, he closed his eyes, anticipating the moment when he riled her just enough to see her anger flare into full-on passion. Confident that day was close, he relaxed into the couch and succumbed to exhaustion.

Chapter 10

Tristan trudged through the dense woods toward the small cabin he'd built. He felt it best to have a refuge outside the walls where he could store supplies and ammunition on the small chance Luthor discovered his true intentions. After unlocking multiple locks on the front door, he stepped inside, sliding the three deadbolts he'd installed into place.

Striding over to the wooden table that doubled as his desk, he sat down to study the documents strewn across it. He pulled the folded notes from his pocket and smoothed them out next to others he'd collected. Studying them, his brow furrowed.

He'd compiled a list of all the cryptic phrases and keywords he'd heard over the radio transmissions he'd monitored over the past few months. Eagle. Tomato. Butterfly. All random words that had been transmitted more than a hundred times. They represented a secret code he didn't understand—and Tristan hated not being in the know.

If anyone was planning a rebellion, it should be him. He had close access to Luthor and wanted to murder the bastard. But Tristan's affection for his sister, Jessica, was a weakness, and whoever was organizing the rebellion must know that.

Which meant they knew too much about him. The thought prickled Tristan's spine as he rested his forehead on his steepled fingers, studying the notes but failing to come up with any answers.

There were cryptic spray-painted messages all over the city if you chose to look. Many of them called for Cromwell's ouster—or even his death—and they were quickly cleaned up by the sanitation crews Luthor employed. Tristan knew Luthor was afraid that if enough people saw them, they'd get the idea a revolution was possible.

Nothing terrified Luthor more than the thought of losing the power he'd so unscrupulously gained.

Releasing a sigh at his inability to discover who was behind the secret transmissions and spray-painted messages, Tristan stacked everything on the desk and prepared to head back inside the city. After bolting up the cabin, he returned to the vulnerable spot in the wall, noticing the two soldiers who lay unconscious on the ground with darts in their necks.

"Idiots," Tristan muttered, sliding through the tear in the metal wall before pushing the two slabs back together. He lifted his watch to his wrist as he approached the Jeep he'd left parked about half a mile away. "You can unloop the cameras now," he said into the smart watch.

A text appeared on the face that read **10-4.**

Bodie, the tech genius Tristan paid handsomely for his help and silence, was a valuable asset to Tristan's agenda. He'd tasked him to surveil for rebellion chatter on what remained of the internet and chat boards, but so far, he'd come up dry.

After all, the internet was a shell of what it used to be. The majority of residents in the city were hooked on EverLife and embroiled in a constant cycle of injecting the drug and then purchasing Luthor's watered-down antidote. Social media no longer existed. The shell government controlled the infrastructure and cell towers, so it made sense people were communicating over radio.

Tristan was just pissed he wasn't part of the communication.

Ten minutes later, he parked in the overgrown field across from his townhome in the inner part of DC. He made sure his bag was zipped before heading inside. Raquel would be there, and he didn't want her discovering the radio from Arthur Reyes.

In fact, he didn't want her to know Arianna and Dominic were in the city at all. The persistent little scientist might try to find her sister, and Tristan wanted her to remain focused on her work for Luthor. That would keep Raquel busy while the lab was destroyed.

Tristan had been glib in his conversation with them earlier, but having Arianna and Dominic destroy Dr. Ziegler's lab was imperative. They had a small window to defeat Cromwell before he became invincible, and having a shit ton of synthetically grown super soldiers wasn't an option.

Tristan was quiet as he locked the door. Raquel's soft snores emanated from the living room where she slept on his pull-out couch. She'd been a rather unassuming houseguest so far, leaving early each morning for the lab and returning around seven o'clock each evening. They rarely interacted—after all, Tristan wasn't looking to make friends. But Raquel reminded him slightly of Jessica, and sheltering the woman in his home would prevent her from ending up like Jess had.

Sucking off a deranged demagogue just to get her hands on more EverLife.

Rubbing his chest as he trudged up the stairs, Tristan acknowledged the burn from the knowledge that Jessica was lost. Even if he killed Cromwell, she wouldn't get back the years she'd lost to addiction and pain.

And still, knowing that, Tristan wanted to try and save her. Hell, he wanted to save everyone from living in the world Luthor Cromwell had created. Sandwiching his hands between his head and the pillow, he lay in bed and stared at the darkened ceiling, hoping like hell he could start the war he wanted. Even if the rebellion wanted nothing to do with him.

In the end, Tristan was convinced that war was the only way to take Cromwell down and defeat the loyalists in the army that now revered him.

And in the chaos of war, Tristan would finally be able to murder the bastard.

Half-thrilled and half-ashamed at the pleasure that thought gave him, he closed his eyes and focused on the darkness behind his lids.

Chapter 11

Arianna awoke to a few sore muscles in her neck, courtesy of the lumpy pillow that would take some getting used to. Guilt gnawed at her that Dominic had slept on the couch, so she decided to scrounge up some breakfast for them. They had some rations in their bags, but she remembered seeing an awning with the word DELI scrawled on it at the end of the block. If she was lucky, it might just be open and serving hot breakfast.

Dominic lay sprawled on the couch, one arm over his eyes as he snored. Snickering at the deep sounds, she tiptoed out of the room and down the stairs. The sun was bright as she made her way onto the sidewalk, and she lifted her face to the sky to soak in the rays.

Small pleasures like warm breakfasts ordered on a whim hadn't existed in Arianna's world for some time. Although she was thankful for the chickens and garden at the farmhouse they'd inhabited in Virginia, eating the same thing every day wasn't exactly titillating. When she neared the deli, she inhaled the delicious aroma that emanated from the building, closing her eyes to savor the smell. A bell rang above as she pushed open the door and entered.

A middle-aged Black woman stood behind a counter ringing up orders as a tall Black man cooked at the grill behind her. Closing the cash register, she smiled and asked, "What'll it be?"

"Two bacon, egg and cheese sandwiches on a bagel if you have them."

"Coming right up," the woman said with a nod.

Arianna's mouth watered as she waited, anticipating the hot, fresh food. She hadn't had a bagel in ages.

"I'm new to the neighborhood," she said, craning her neck to watch the cook crack open the eggs on the grill. "It's nice to see you all are in business since so many stores are boarded up."

"Name's Deandra," the woman said before gesturing her head toward the cook. "And that's my husband, Ron. We never touched EverLife and just kept making food once the world collapsed. We live upstairs and stay in our own little corner of heaven." She arched a sardonic eyebrow. "As long as we don't bother anyone, we do just fine."

"Do you still get food deliveries? I notice there's not really any traffic. Not like there used to be, anyway."

Crossing her arms, she leaned on the counter behind the register. "How long have you been gone? Things have changed a lot here since Luthor Cromwell closed off the city. We still have some technology, but it's sparse. And I keep chickens, pigs and a garden in the back. Food distributors kind of fell by the wayside when EverLife took over society."

"I bet," Arianna said, admiring her resiliency. "Looks like you figured it out."

"For now." Ron wrapped the sandwiches and dropped them beside the register. Deandra placed them in a brown paper bag before tapping a few keys on the register. "That will be $27.50."

"Wow." Arianna pulled thirty bucks from her pocket and handed it over.

"Inflation is the name of the game around here," she said, stuffing the money in the register drawer before closing it. "We're open seven days a week so stop by anytime."

Leaning in, Arianna lowered her voice. "I also noticed some messages of dissention spray-painted around town. You know anything about that?"

Deandra lifted her brows. "Information costs a lot more than the sandwiches. How much you got?"

Chuckling at her candor, Arianna straightened. "Not enough for today, but I'll be back. Name's Arianna. See ya." With a salute, she exited, ready to devour the hot sandwiches.

When she entered the hotel room, she locked the deadbolt before turning and calling Dominic's name. Walking through the tiny foyer, she saw him rise from the couch, his boots haphazardly thrown on but only one actually tied.

"Dom?"

Pacing toward her, he gripped her upper arms and squeezed so tightly it reminded her of the tourniquet the nurses used to wrap when they needed to draw blood for her army physicals. Bristling, she asked, "What the hell—?"

"Goddamnit, woman," Dominic exclaimed, his fingers digging into her skin. "I'm going to fucking strangle you."

Dominic stared at Arianna's stunned expression as fury bubbled in his chest. When he'd woken up to find her gone, he'd immediately transitioned to full-blown panic mode. He'd been in the process of hastily tying his boots when she entered.

"Do you not understand the meaning of 'we're a team?' Did you even think about telling me where the hell you were going?"

"Okay, *Dad*," she scoffed, backing away from the death grip he had on her arms and holding up a bag. "I went to the end of the block to get breakfast. We both have to eat, right?"

"This isn't about me keeping tabs on you," he said, frustrated at his overreaction, but needing her to understand it was unacceptable for her to continue insisting on doing everything on her own. "We're each other's only ally in this city, Ari. You can't disappear without telling me."

"Jesus," she muttered, tossing the bag on the cheap coffee table and throwing up her hands. "I'm a big girl, Dom. I can walk to the end of the street without your help."

Clenching his fists, Dominic looked to the ceiling and prayed for patience. "Don't do it again. I mean it, Arianna. If you even think of leaving my presence, I want to know. Otherwise, I can't protect you."

"I don't need protecting," she said through clenched teeth.

"I don't give a shit what you think you need. I won't be the one who returns to Arthur's compound and tells Dani her sister is dead because I wasn't there to help her. Don't leave my sight again without telling me."

She scoffed, red splotches appearing on her cheeks as her eyes flashed with anger. "God forbid you have to disappoint your *precious* Dani." Pivoting, she stomped toward the bedroom and slammed the door.

Emitting a curse, Dominic lowered to the couch and rubbed a harsh hand over his face. He immediately realized he'd handled the situation terribly, but he'd been terrified when he'd woken up to find her gone. He'd just gone into military mode, determined to find her.

Now that he had a moment to gather his thoughts, he pondered why his reaction had been one of pure terror.

Probably because they'd reached the point where she was starting to let him in. She'd accepted his offer to be friends, and if he had it his way, soon they'd cross the line to lovers. He was man enough to admit that he wanted her, not just her body—although he certainly wanted every inch of her tanned skin pressed against his. But more importantly, he wanted her openness. Her trust.

Her...*love*.

Yes, he knew that somewhere deep inside that hard shell, Arianna loved him. He'd seen the sentiment clearly in her face in that moment in the lab when the world had stood still. Nothing had mattered but the emotion shining in the woman's eyes who he'd finally seen for the very first time.

And damn it, he wanted to see that emotion again.

Of course, he couldn't see anything if she was dead, which was why her little disappearing act had ruffled his usually controlled feathers.

Sighing, he picked up the bag and opened it, closing his eyes as he inhaled the smell of bacon and eggs. Removing one of the foil-wrapped sandwiches, he walked to the bedroom door and knocked.

She pulled it open a few seconds later, glaring at him with annoyance and frustration. Lifting the sandwich, he flashed a grin. "Peace offering?"

She snatched the sandwich from his hand before slamming the door in his face. Dominic's lips twitched at her obstinance. Returning to the couch, he opened the remaining sandwich and ate in silence.

Arianna eventually strode into the living room, planting her fists on her hips as she stared at him. "I'm sorry," she finally said, surprising Dominic as his eyes widened. "I didn't want to wake you. I didn't even think you'd be worried about me. I'm not used to having people care that I'm gone."

He released a deflated breath. "I care."

Her gaze lowered to the floor as her throat bobbed. "And I know you don't want to bring Dani bad news. She's important—"

"So are you," he interrupted, rising and coming to stand in front of her. "And I'm getting pretty tired of you twisting everything I say to make it about Dani. This is about *you*, Arianna."

"You're the one who brought her up—"

"Stop," he said, shaking his head. "Just stop. Honestly, I think it's time we stopped hiding in general and really started talking. I'm done pretending nothing happened in the lab."

Her eyes clouded with fear, and Dominic's heart cracked at the intense doubt and pain there. Just the mere mention of discussing her feelings seemed to terrify her. Man, they really were a pair of broken souls. Both afraid to acknowledge the emotion that roared within because love had been disastrously painful for both of them.

"Arianna—"

"Not yet," she said, holding up a hand. "I'm just..." She shook her head. "Not yet. But I'm sorry about leaving without telling you. I won't do it again."

The corner of Dominic's lip ticked up. "Did I just get a concession from you?"

She arched an eyebrow, the move sexy enough to send a jolt of desire through his frame. Fuck, she was absolutely gorgeous when she let those shields down and actually smiled at him.

"Yes. Don't blow it by being a dumbass, okay?"

Laughing, he exhaled a short breath. "Okay."

"Now, if you're done berating me, let me tell you about Deandra. She owns the deli and I think we can get some information from her—if we pay up."

Intrigued, Dominic gestured toward the couch. "I'm all ears. After that, we can plan our surveillance tactic for Dr. Ziegler's lab. We'll want to scope it out at night to retain cover. In the meantime, we can try and track down your old contacts and see if they have any intel on the possible rebellion."

Lowering to the couch, her face lit with excitement. "Sounds like a plan. The first thing I noticed about Deandra was the knowledge lurking in her eyes. I'm pretty sure she sees everything that happens on this block. And perhaps even farther than that..."

Chapter 12

Once Arianna caught Dominic up on her visit to the deli, they sifted over Tristan's map, studying the details of Dr. Ziegler's lab.

"It seems pretty straightforward," Dominic said, eyebrows drawn together as he traced the map with his finger. "It's a one-story warehouse and the lab is in the middle. We can enter through this back door, and if we light the explosives here"—he tapped the map—"that will give us time to exit before the lab explodes."

"Tristan labeled every spot where the guards stand at their posts," Arianna said, noting each X drawn on the map. "He also indicated each of the two guards at the back door take a bathroom break each night at midnight and one a.m. respectively. So, if we break in and blow up the lab at midnight, we'll only have to disarm one guard."

He nodded as he calculated the steps of the mission in his head.

"And we still have two tranquilizer darts left. Hopefully, we can do this without killing anyone. I think we can surveil tonight to confirm the timing and carry out the mission tomorrow if everything checks out."

"Agreed."

"In the meantime, I'm not content to sit around and wait for Tristan to lead me to Raquel. I want to approach my contacts and see if they know where he lives or anything about the rebellion."

"Okay. Are you sure they're still in DC?"

"Not at all," she said, lifting a shoulder. "But there's only one way to find out."

Two hours later, they navigated to the Columbia Heights section of the city. Arianna led Dominic through the parking lot of an abandoned Target superstore before they crossed to the next block. It was lined with brick apartment buildings and appeared quite normal in the chaos that now consumed the world.

"Pretty nice street," Dominic said thoughtfully. "It looks like someone is maintaining the cherry blossom trees."

Arianna observed the row of manicured trees in front of several of the buildings. "Guess some people try to hold on to a semblance of normalcy even if the world has turned to shit. Gotta love the optimism."

"I feel like I'm in a quasi-reality," he said, shaking his head. "It's still DC, but it's so...quiet."

The rumble of an engine echoed in the distance before growing louder. Arianna's gaze swung to Dominic before they jetted behind a large oak tree. Resting her palm on the bark, she craned her neck, observing a large tank meander down the street. Two black military-style Jeeps followed behind, causing the hairs on the back of her neck to stand up.

"A show of power from Cromwell?" Dominic asked softly.

"Probably. Never thought I'd see tanks on the streets of DC, but this is where we're at."

They waited until the vehicles disappeared before resuming their walk. Eventually, Arianna halted in front of a building with an awning that read The Stalwart, and pointed toward the top of the building. "He lives on the fourth floor. Or he used to. We'll see."

The lock on the door that led to the lobby was broken, so they slipped inside and eyed the elevator. "I'm not getting on that thing," Arianna said, grimacing at the dilapidated buttons and graffiti on the elevator doors. "Let's take the stairs."

Dominic followed her, acknowledging he was perfectly content to always allow her to lead him up any flight of stairs. Watching her ass sway was quickly becoming his favorite pastime.

When they reached the fourth floor, each breathing a bit heavier, Arianna stopped before the door labeled 412. She knocked and waited, glancing at him as something shuffled behind the door.

It swung open revealing a tall man with brown tousled hair wearing a pair of boxer shorts. Thin legs extended to bare feet, and he rubbed his chest, which was smattered with small patches of scraggly hair. Confusion clouded his sleep-filled eyes as he asked, "Arianna?"

"Hey, Matt. Long time."

"I'll say. Uh, what are you doing here?"

A woman appeared behind Matt, wrapped in a robe with a surprised expression. "Ari?"

"Hey, Susan. Guess you two are still together. Saves me from tracking you down separately."

Matt shook his head in rapid movements as if trying to snap back to reality. "I thought you were dead."

"No such luck," she said, patting him on the arm and breezing inside. "Throw on some clothes and I'll tell you where I've been. Then I'm going to need to pick both your brains."

"I'm Dominic," he said, thrusting out his hand. "I've heard absolutely nothing about you."

"Oh, where are my manners?" Arianna asked, plastering on a fake smile as she blinked rapidly. "Dominic, meet Matt. My former fiancé."

Dominic couldn't have been more floored if the building collapsed beneath their feet. Fiancé? He hadn't realized she'd ever been engaged. Especially to a scrawny guy like this who she could've chewed up and spit out in a matter of seconds. "Nice to meet you."

"Uh, yeah. You too, man. This is Susan. We'll toss on some clothes and be right back."

Arianna snooped around the living room, looking at the framed pictures on the shelf as they waited.

"Your contact is your former fiancé?" Dominic finally asked.

"Yeah, so what? He pretended to love me so I'd promote him—and it worked. Last time we spoke, he had top level security clearance, so it would be stupid to let our past interfere with any intelligence I can gather."

"You could've told me," he said, eyebrows drawing together.

"Why? It doesn't matter. Besides, he owes me."

"For what?"

"For fucking Susan while we were engaged."

Dominic allowed the uncomfortable feelings surge as Matt and Susan reentered the room. Anger Arianna hadn't told him they were approaching her ex. Annoyance at her implied indifference that Matt cheated on her. Jealousy that the man had ever touched her. His eyes raked over Matt's lanky frame. *This* guy had seduced Arianna? Dominic could barely believe it. He wasn't nearly...*enough* for her.

Matt led them to the couch, and Arianna sat down, rubbing her thighs before speaking.

"So, you're still in this dump?"

Breathing a laugh, Matt rubbed his forehead. "Still a ball buster. Yes, we managed to stay inside the city and stay clear of EverLife...for the most part," he said, eyeing Susan.

"Hey, everyone was taking it," she said with a guilty shrug. "I was curious. But thank god I only tried the pills and never injected the shit. My stomach hurt terribly after the first dose, and I was pissed at the side effects. Later, I realized how lucky I was that I couldn't tolerate it."

"And I never tried it," Matt said, leaning back and lacing his hands behind his head. "I mean, I look young enough anyway."

Arianna rolled her eyes. "I can see your ego's still intact. But more importantly, do you still have security clearance?"

"I have some," he said, shaking his foot as it crossed over his knee. "Luthor Cromwell assigned me as bodyguard to his socialite niece. He has a soft spot for her, and she's not the brightest twenty-four-year-old I've ever met. Since his family members are targets, he wants her protected."

"So, you left the army."

"More like transferred. Luthor required an oath of loyalty when he took over as commander once President Johnson overdosed on EverLife. I had no desire to pledge it, and we were going to leave the city." He reached over and clasped Susan's hand. "But I had an acquaintance who told me about the security job and helped me land it."

"This acquaintance must be close to Luthor," Arianna said.

"Tristan works for him, yes."

Dominic spared a glance at Arianna. "He's got his hands in everything, hmm?"

"You know Tristan?" Matt asked.

"Yeah. In fact, Raquel is staying with him. Do you know where he lives?"

"Raquel is in the city?" Matt sat forward, resting his forearms on his thighs. "I had no idea. I don't know where Tristan lives, but I can certainly find out."

"That would be helpful. We're here to rescue her. I don't want to divulge the details, but she made some bad decisions and we're afraid for her safety."

"Is she one of the new scientists working for Luthor?" Matt asked, rubbing his chin. "I heard Selena mention there were a few new members added to the antidote development team."

"Yes," Dominic said, assuming Selena was Luthor's niece.

"Well, that's a development." Matt arched a brow. "What else do you need?"

"We want to uncover information on the possible rebellion that's forming. It's obvious from the cryptic messages spray-painted across the city that dissention is brewing."

"Something is brewing, but I'm not on the inside. I keep to myself and focus on doing my job. It seems the best path to not getting myself killed."

Dominic's nostrils flared as annoyance surged. Ol' Matt seemed like a bona fide pussy, and he couldn't believe he'd ever laid a hand on Arianna. Had she actually been pleased by this guy?

"And do you still work for Colonel McGrath?" Arianna asked Susan. "He was high-ranking enough that you had access to classified information. We'd like to know about the top-secret lab where Dr. Ziegler is developing the soldier-enhancing drug."

"No one's supposed to know about that," Susan said, fear flashing in her eyes as they widened. "Who told you?"

"Your buddy Tristan. He's annoying as hell but knows a lot of secret shit. I wasn't sure whether to believe him, but it seems he was telling the truth."

"Sadly, he is," Susan said, slowly tracing the couch with her fingers. "Many people I work with are terrified at the thought of a super-powered drug created to enhance soldiers' strength."

"So you do still work for him?"

Her cheeks puffed as she exhaled a breath. "Yes. Colonel McGrath pledged loyalty to Luthor, and although I still work for him, it's not like it used to be before the city was walled off. The internet is controlled by Luthor's hackers, so my executive assistant duties have been diminished. I mostly ensure the colonel receives any transmissions or secure emails sent by Luthor or his generals, and water the plants." She shrugged. "I'm getting paid in cash now that the banks collapsed, but I'm not sure how long that will last. There are grumblings that Luthor is going to create his own currency."

"Even though the city has technology, it seems like it's not really accessible," Dominic said.

"It's not." Rising, Susan walked to the kitchen and returned with a smart watch. "This stopped updating months ago, and many of my friends have noticed the same with their phones and tablets. Luthor is slowly cutting off technology to those of us in the city who aren't in his inner circle. Thankfully, Matt's phone still works since it's part of his security package for Luthor's niece. Luthor only allows one cell phone company to exist within the walls, and it's too expensive for people outside of his affluent circle to afford the service."

Leaning back, Arianna crossed one booted foot over the other. "Do you think that's why a rebellion is forming?"

"People certainly hate losing access to technology," she said, "but I think the more pressing issue is that people in the city are beginning to see the truth. Luthor has been clear that maintaining power is his ultimate goal. He'll surround himself with people who have the wealth and connections to make that happen."

"And he'll have no regard for anyone else," Dominic said.

"Exactly."

Matt leaned back, stretching his arm across the back of the couch as he spoke. "Even though I want no part of the rebellion—I mean, I like living, thank you very much—I do think the people who aren't in Luthor's inner circle will try to challenge him. It's going to be tough without any weapons or technology."

"Not if they have backing from the compounds beyond the city walls," Arianna said, cocking an eyebrow.

Straightening, Matt's gaze grew serious. "Is that a possibility? I thought all the compounds were filled with addicts and crime."

"Because that's what Luthor wants you to think." Tilting her head, Arianna asked, "If you had to track down Raquel, where is the first place you'd look? Tristan says he's going to lead us to her eventually, but I'm not putting all my eggs in that basket."

Matt's expression turned contemplative. "Probably at Luthor's black tie birthday party tomorrow. Many of his officers will be in attendance, along with his acquaintances. I would imagine he'd invite the scientists to tout the development of his precious drugs."

Arianna looked at Dominic, and he saw the unmistakable glow of sisterly concern in her eyes. "If that's the case, we should try to infiltrate the party before blowing up the lab. Maybe we can find Raquel without having to do Tristan's bidding."

"We should still scope out the lab tonight just in case," Dominic said. "But I'm open to waiting on blowing it up if we can gain access to the party."

"I can get you on the list," Susan said. "That's something I can still access from Colonel McGrath's office."

"Excellent." Rising, she pointed between them. "I wasn't sure you'd come in handy when I found out my fiancé was fucking my commanding officer's assistant. But it seems it all worked out in the end, hmm?"

Standing, Matt opened his hands in a shrug. "That was ages ago, Ari. And it was for the best, wasn't it? We were never right for each other."

"It probably was since you fucked me just to get promoted. You got what you wanted and now you both can do me some favors for being huge dicks. So, yeah, I guess it was worth it." Facing Dominic, she jerked her head toward the door. "Come on. Let's allow these two to get to work. I want the location of Tristan's apartment and access to Luthor's birthday party by tomorrow morning."

She stomped toward the door and Dominic followed her, aware of the swirling emotions deep in his gut. Arianna was a master at appearing indifferent, but he understood it was just a mask. A very complicated, impenetrable mask. Inside, she was clearly hurting at the reminder of Matt and Susan's betrayal, and he desperately wanted to comfort her.

Of course, he'd learned long ago that trying to comfort Arianna when she had those walls up was like trying to get two rattlesnakes to cuddle. The chances were between zero and none.

"Arianna?" Susan called, following them to the door and wrapping her arm around Matt's waist. "For what it's worth, I'm really sorry. You didn't deserve the way we both treated you."

"You're right," Arianna said, opening the door and crossing the threshold. "And I don't need an apology. I need information and action. I'll be back tomorrow morning and expect everything to be ready. Don't make me get grumpy. Neither of you want to see that."

Dominic's lips twitched as he stifled a laugh at the fact the woman was always grumpy. But she was right. They seemed smart enough to understand it would be easier to help her than to get on the wrong side of her trigger finger.

"I need more time than that, Ari," Matt said.

With a frustrated huff, she pivoted. "That deadline is firm." Resting her hand on the butt of the gun strapped to her hip, she arched an eyebrow. "Are we clear?"

Matt's throat bobbed as he eyed the gun. "We're clear."

With a nod, Arianna descended the stairs.

"He's scared shitless of you," Dominic remarked as he followed behind her.

"Yep. I think he always was."

When they reached the lobby, Dominic encircled her wrist, drawing her to a halt. "There's no way in hell that guy did it for you, Arianna. What did you see in him?"

An almost wistful smile played with her stunning lips as she contemplated. "For a moment, I think I saw normalcy. Acceptance. And maybe a hint of love."

Dominic's features scrunched with disbelief, and she laughed. "But you're right, he was terrible in bed. I almost feel sorry for Susan." Lifting a finger, she grinned. "Almost."

Chuckling, Dominic shook his head. "Wow. You're really over it. I guess that's admirable, although I'd still be pissed."

Her shoulders deflated slightly as she kicked the ground with the toe of her boot. "It's pointless to get riled up over something you were never meant to have in the first place. I realize that now."

Dominic studied her as she stared at the ground, not meeting his gaze. "You deserve love, Arianna. I'm sorry you stopped believing that somewhere along the way. I'm even sorrier that asshole reinforced the belief." He jutted his finger toward the stairs. "He's not even close to worthy of you."

Her eyes finally met his, filled with a soft vulnerability that he'd rarely seen—jolting his heart into overdrive as energy pulsed between them.

And then it was gone, replaced with the hard steel and cool collectiveness that usually resided in her green-brown flecked orbs. "You're right. He's a fucking douche, but I'll take his help, and Susan's too."

She strode onto the sunlit street, waving him along as she set a brisk pace. "Now, come on. I need to know where to find a dress for this fancy party, and I bet Deandra can help me. I want your opinion on her and Ron."

Thrilled that she'd openly admitted she wanted his assessment, he fell into step beside her and headed back to LeDroit Park.

CHAPTER 13

D ani trudged through the forest, scanning the shrub-
bery as her husband trailed behind. Thankful for his
protection—and the other three men Arthur had tasked to
come with them—she crouched to examine a plant with
dark green leaves.

"Holy shit," she breathed, touching the hairless, pointed
leaf. "It's a milk thistle."

Maverick lowered beside her, eyebrows drawn together
as he studied it.

"See the white marbling on the leaves? That's where it
gets the 'milk' moniker from."

"Thrilling stuff," Maverick teased.

Swatting his chest, she laughed. "Do you know what this
means, Mav? I've got them all! All the plants I need to
replicate the serum. I mean, I think I do," she said, rubbing
her forehead. "We'll only know once I test it on the mice
we inject with EverLife, and if that works, on the patients
in the clinic."

"What do you need me to do?"

Dani gazed at the man she'd woken up beside that morning, recalling the ardent pounding of her heart. She'd read
a note in her own handwriting that informed her to watch
several videos on a smart phone, and Maverick had laid still
beside her as she viewed them.

As the videos progressed, a sense of *knowing* had washed
over her. Like she'd watched them countless times and

she was safe. Afterward, she'd rolled over and cupped her husband's jaw.

"Champagne," she whispered, running her thumb along his stubble. "We used to drink champagne together, didn't we?"

His expression shone with love as he nodded. "You're remembering things faster every day, slugger. I'm proud of you."

Blood pounded in Dani's frame as she accepted her intense attraction to a man she didn't remember but who her body very much recognized. The yearning to reach for him and wrap herself around his muscled body thrummed through every cell.

"Not yet, my naughty little geneticist," he said, kissing the tip of her nose. "We've got plants to hunt today. But tonight, all bets are off." He'd arched a sexy eyebrow before sliding out of bed, leaving her rapt with anticipation of revisiting the conversation once the day was over.

Returning to the moment, she wiped her hands on her pants and rose. "I need you and the men to extricate all the plants you see with the white marbling. We'll plant some in one of the overgrown areas behind the school. It's invasive, so we don't want to plant it in the garden."

"Got it," Maverick said with a salute.

"I'll remove the leaves when we get back to the compound and start testing combinations with the other plants immediately."

"Is it weird that I'm slightly turned on by you discussing plant combinations?"

Tossing her head back, she laughed. "Yes, it's very weird. Also, remind me to write this moment in my journal. Even if I don't always remember, it's times like these that I understand how easily I must've fallen for you. That killer smile and sense of humor must've knocked me off my feet."

"You never stood a chance," he said, leaning in to peck her lips. "Plus, I'm amazing in bed."

Mirth danced in Dani's heart as she gazed into his gunmetal gray eyes. She made a mental note to document this moment in her journal for the days her memories were scarcer. Some days were better than others, according to her notes, but her journal held a plethora of information about her husband.

"I have a lot of reminders in my journal to tell you I love you," she said softly. "That it makes you really happy when I say it back."

"Only if you mean it, sweetheart," he said, tucking a strand of hair behind her ear. "I don't want to push you."

Swallowing thickly, she whispered. "I love you. I feel it so deeply right here." She rubbed her fingers over her heart.

"Babe," he murmured, sliding an arm around her waist. "Keep telling me that and I'm going to ravish you in a pile of milk thistle."

Wrinkling her nose, she drew back. "That would be really uncomfortable, but I appreciate the effort."

Maverick winked before calling the other men over. After giving instructions, they gripped their shears and shovels and began to dig up the plants.

Dani watched them work, hope welling in her heart that she was close to a cure. The crushing weight of guilt lodged in her throat, and she joined the others, shoveling the dirt away with firm resolve. Reveling in the burn her muscles experienced from the manual labor, she silently envisioned saving the world from the destruction she'd wrought.

Chapter 14

That evening, long past sunset, Arianna and Dominic stood on the hill above the Dr. Ziegler's lab. They'd walked almost two hours to get to Glover Park, the neighborhood where the lab resided.

Dominic crouched behind the trunk of the large tree, peeking around the right side as Arianna scouted from her perch to his left.

"Two guards as we expected," she said, eyes narrowed as she gazed into the distance. "It will be midnight soon. Let's confirm they take breaks as Tristan indicated."

Dominic nodded, palm pressed to the rough bark as they waited. Sure enough, at the stroke of midnight, one of the guards disappeared inside.

"The lab isn't as big as the one we infiltrated to get Dani's antidote," Arianna said. "We should be able to breach it and light the explosives quickly."

"Unless we run into extra guards inside we didn't anticipate. If Cromwell really is working on a drug that powerful, you'd think he'd have more than two guards outside."

Arianna shot him a droll look. "Or he might just be arrogant enough to believe no one would challenge him. Power can make a man drunk with overconfidence."

"True." Standing, Dominic gripped the strap of the rifle slung behind his back. "I think we've gotten the surveillance we need. I'd be worried to enter a mission on such little prep time with anyone but you, but I know we can knock this out."

She seemed pleased at his praise, causing warmth to spread through his frame. A satisfied smile flirted with her lips as she rose. "Well then, I guess it's time to head back to our shitty hotel. I have to say, I miss cars. Maybe we can find a damn bike or something. Walking is good conditioning but not the most practical method of transportation."

"You're telling me," Dominic said, feeling exhaustion set in at the nearly four-mile walk ahead. They would get back to the motel around two a.m., and at least he could get several hours of sleep before Arianna woke him up for their morning jog.

"Speaking of conditioning," she said as they trudged through the quiet neighborhood. "How's your injury?" She tapped her neck where it met her shoulder. "Haven't heard you complain, which is really fucking cool. I'm glad you're not a pansy."

Breathing a laugh, he rubbed the slightly puffy scar. "It feels good today. Dani said the bullet hit the optimal place for me to bleed profusely but otherwise not suffer any long-term damage."

"Lucky bastard." She flashed a grin. "If they ever reinstate the lottery, you should play."

"Only if you coach me. I'm convinced our morning training sessions helped. I appreciate you taking the time to help me condition."

"What the hell else was I going to do?" she asked, shrugging as her boots stomped the grass in the field they entered along the path. "There's nothing to do on Arthur's compound except figure out how to save the world. And Dani's got that covered."

"I think we're all doing our little part." Glancing at her out of the corner of his eye, he asked, "Are we going to talk about Matt and Susan? Or is that subject closed?"

"There's really nothing to talk about. We met when I was his commanding officer, dated, became engaged. You know, all the shit normal people are supposed to want. Then I found out he was fucking Susan, and we got in a huge argument where he basically admitted he was with me to advance his career."

Dominic let that settle in, understanding how much it must've hurt to hear those words.

"He said it just like that? What a dick."

"Just like that," she said with a nod. "But I appreciated the honesty. It was nice to finally get some from him."

Pursing his lips, Dominic reminded himself to tread lightly. "Something like that would make it hard to trust a man again or to even want to be in a relationship."

"It wasn't the first time," she said flippantly. "My college boyfriend cheated on me with my roommate. There's something about me that makes men stick their dicks in other women. Not sure what it is, but I'm smart enough to stop repeating the same actions and expecting different results."

"Or you could've just dated jerks who weren't ready for a woman like you."

She scoffed. "Yeah, maybe. Anyway"—she waved a dismissive hand—"that's all there is to the story. If you're in a mood to talk, you can tell me about Pam. What was her favorite song?"

Joy rippled through him at the question. It was a thoughtful one that no one had ever asked about his sister. "'Make You Feel My Love,'" he said, his voice gravelly as emotion welled. "The Garth Brooks version. Pam loved Garth."

"That's a good one. What was her favorite food?"

They continued on for several minutes, Arianna asking questions about his sister that caused fond memories to swell—along with the painful ones.

"Her favorite movie was *Love, Actually*," he said, his boots quiet on the sidewalk in the tree-lined neighborhood they were currently crossing. "She loved that scene where the girl sang the Mariah Carey song."

"If you tell anyone I admitted this, I'll deny it, but that Mariah Carey Christmas song is dope. I'm a sucker for it."

Dominic made an X over his heart. "It's in the vault. Music can bring out something in a person's soul. On Pam's last day, she asked me to play 'Make You Feel My Love' for her.

She said she wanted to hear Garth and imagine what it would be like to fall in love one last time. I'll never forget her expression as she lay in the bed, eyes closed and a huge smile on her face. She was so happy." He cleared his throat as his vision blurred from the tears that stung his eyes.

"Mom was the same way," Arianna said, her tone solemn. "Not with a song, but she took my hand and said the sweetest things to me. Then she closed her eyes and squeezed my wrist. She was very weak and it must've taken a lot of strength. When she opened them..." Her throat bobbed in the moonlight as she paused. "She looked at me with so much love. More than anyone in my life ever had. It was...beautiful...and peaceful."

"Those last moments are special. I can see why Raquel was upset she didn't get to say goodbye to your mom, although she had a pretty shitty way of making you pay for it."

"I'll say. I'm going to give her hell once I rescue her."

Entranced by the ease of their conversation, Dominic fought the urge to reach over and grasp her hand. They were sharing intimate details about meaningful and private moments in their lives, which he knew Arianna rarely did. It moved something deep within, and he realized he craved *more*.

More intimacy with her. More glimpses of that soft smile instead of the harsh frown. More moments where it was just the two of them, comfortable and open.

A loud snap sounded behind them and Dominic whirled around, slinging his rifle over his shoulder and assessing the darkened surroundings. Were they being followed?

Arianna did the same, feet firmly planted as she held the rifle to her shoulder, aiming in the distance.

"Do you see anything?" she whispered.

"No, but that doesn't mean no one's there. Stay alert."

They began to slowly back down the street, still facing the direction where the sound originated. A gun cocked to Dominic's left, and he snapped his head. He saw the flash of dark metal before a Sen Force soldier appeared from behind a tree.

"Run!" he shouted to Arianna, and they began a full-on sprint down the sidewalk toward the nearby woods. Bullets whizzed past their heads as they ran before darting behind a brick apartment building. Dominic spotted a large metal dumpster and called to Arianna.

"Take cover!"

They crouched behind the dumpster, breathless as Dominic assessed the situation.

"I spotted four men," he said, lifting his eyebrows for confirmation.

"Same. Do you think they followed us from the lab or they were out on patrol?"

"Not sure, but I saw the Sen Force badge on their uniforms." The Sen Force logo had replaced all other insignia on US military uniforms when Luthor Cromwell seized control of the government.

"Our best bet is to draw them in so we can line up our shots. I can lure them toward us, and you can take them out."

"I can advance while you stay here. You're healing and I'm in better condition—"

"No," he said, his voice firm as he cut her off. "You stay here and aim for their necks as I draw them in."

A muscle ticked in her jaw. "Stop trying to be a fucking hero, Dom—"

"Not up for discussion. Stay sharp." Before she could argue, he straightened and emerged from behind the dumpster.

The Sen Force soldiers immediately spotted him and advanced, and he sprayed bullets from his rifle, confident Arianna would systematically take them out. Sure enough, a bullet fired from the darkness behind the dumpster, lodging in one soldier's throat. He gasped and clutched the wound before falling to the ground.

Another man behind him lowered to check his pulse, and Arianna took the opportunity to shoot him in the lower back. He collapsed atop the other soldier, his body limp.

The remaining two soldiers wised up and hid behind the bricks on the far side of the nearby building. Rejoining

Arianna behind the dumpster, Dom spoke in short, clipped words.

"Good job," he said, frustrated at his erratic breathing. "I'm going to advance on the remaining two. When I draw them out, shoot them."

"Not this time," she said, crossing behind him and craning her neck to look down the sidewalk to where the other men hid. "I'm advancing and you shoot."

"No." He circled her wrist, drawing her back. "I won't let you—"

"It's not your choice." Yanking her wrist from his grasp, she whisked onto the street and began advancing.

"Stubborn fucking woman," he muttered, fury lacing with fear that she would put herself in danger, especially when he was the one who should protect her.

It was an antiquated thought for a woman as tough and progressive as Arianna, but hell, Dominic was old school and he protected what was his.

And Arianna was *his*, goddamnit.

As soon as they finished taking down the bastards who were hunting them, he'd make sure she got the message. No more waiting. No more pretending. The present moment showed just how fleeting life could be, and he was done denying there was something between them. Dominic was ready to take action.

But first, he had to ensure they stayed alive.

The first soldier darted out from behind the brick, shooting at Arianna as she strategically advanced between the trees that lined the street. Dominic planted his feet on the sidewalk, lifted his handgun and aimed at the man's forehead. He didn't stand a chance.

His eyes widened before blood began to trickle from the bullet wound. Crumpling to the ground, he exhaled his last breath.

Arianna approached the last soldier as Dominic fought the urge to scream for her to retreat. Terror pulsed through his body at the thought of losing her, and he waited with bated breath for her to draw the last soldier out. When he appeared, Dominic shot him in the thigh. The man grimaced, dropping his weapon to grab the injured flesh, and Dominic took the opportunity to shoot him in the other thigh as well.

He and Arianna both jogged up to the man, who was now rolling around in intense pain on the sidewalk.

"Did you follow us?" Dominic asked, kicking the man in the kidney. "Answer me!"

"We patrol this neighborhood for Sen Force," the soldier said through clenched teeth. "We noticed you walking and hadn't seen you before. I swear, that's it."

"I actually believe him," Arianna said.

The soldier gagged several times before relaxing on the ground, unconscious. Lights began to illuminate the surrounding homes and apartment buildings, and Arianna jerked her head. "Let's go."

They ran out of the neighborhood, following the trail they'd taken earlier to get to the lab. As they made their way back to LeDroit Park, Dominic felt his anger grow from a dull throb to an all-consuming burn. He was pissed Arianna had put herself in danger and could tell she damn well knew it.

"I don't take commands from anyone, Dominic," she said, her tone angry as they moved at a fast pace.

"It's not about taking commands," he spat out. "Your insistence on doing everything on your own is going to get us both killed."

"I told you to stay on Arthur's compound," she gritted. "I work best alone."

Dominic remained silent, worried he was going to say something he couldn't take back. Deciding to shelve the discussion for now, he focused on controlling his seething frustration.

One thing was fucking certain: when they got back to the motel, he was going to lay everything on the table with Arianna and outline new rules. No more solo decision making. They were a team, and she needed to start respecting that.

And when he was done imparting the new rules, he was finally going to take advantage of all that energy that buzzed between them.

Dominic was ready to claim Arianna in all the ways he should have over the years they'd known each other. All the times he'd stupidly overlooked her.

As they trudged through the city, he kept repeating the same phrase in his head.

Tonight, Arianna Lawson is **mine**.

Chapter 15

Arianna could tell Dominic was pissed she hadn't let him take control during the ambush. What he couldn't understand was the surge of abject terror she felt when he stepped onto the sidewalk to draw out the soldiers. Every heart-wrenching scene from the moments he'd been bleeding out on the lab floor had flashed through her brain. It had been the worst moment of Arianna's life—where she was sure she'd lost the love of her damn life—and she wasn't apt to repeat it.

In an effort to prevent him harm, she'd lurched from behind the dumpster to draw out the remaining two soldiers. Hell, she was more than competent and didn't take orders from anyone.

Not even Dominic, no matter how she felt about him.

Anger clouded his features as they entered the lobby of the motel, Devon straightening behind the desk as he yawned. "Hey, guys. Late night—"

"Shut it," Arianna snapped, annoyed at the attempt to chit chat. Not only was she not in the mood for polite conversation, but she was growing more furious by the minute. Dominic was upset at *her*? Annoyed at his entitled anger, she climbed the stairs, ready to shut herself into the bedroom and cool down before they got into an argument.

When they entered the foyer, she stalked to the small kitchen table and removed her weapons. They slammed on the cheap wood with ominous clanks before she returned to the entrance hallway to kick off her boots. Anxious for some solace to gather herself, she turned to walk to the bedroom. Dominic's hand snaked around her wrist, forcing her to halt.

Arianna pivoted, anxious to run from the feelings that pulsed in every cell of her body when he was near. Furious at being manhandled, she attempted to yank her arm from his grasp. "Let go of me!"

Fire flashed in his eyes and a muscle ticked in his jaw. His gaze bore into hers, dark and fierce as he pushed her toward the wall.

"What are you—?"

"Not this time," he said, the arousal-laden timbre of his voice shooting sparks of desire through her frame. "No more running, Ari." Pressing her to the wall, he stepped forward, crowding her. The roof of her mouth turned to dust, dry as sandpaper as his evergreen scent overwhelmed her.

Tilting her head back, she stared into his eyes, determined not to look away. The firm muscles of his pecs brushed her breasts under her functional black t-shirt and bra, and she had to suppress the urge to whimper. God, her nipples were hard. Closing her eyes for the briefest second, she willed away the desire.

Lifting her lids, her nostrils flared as she spoke through clenched teeth. "Let. Me. Go."

He scoffed, the arrogant sound sending fury down her spine. Bristling, she yanked her arm again to no avail.

"You're a damn good fighter, Ari, but you forget one thing," he said, his deep voice gravelly.

"And what is that?" She lifted her chin, defiant under his heated gaze. Every single muscle seemed frozen by the warmth of his strong body.

Labored breaths escaped his lips, although they were nowhere near as frenzied as the choppy pants that exited her lungs.

"I'm bigger than you," he murmured, lifting her wrist above her head and pressing it to the wall. His fingers cinched on the soft flesh there—perhaps one of the softest places on her shaking frame besides the tender skin of her inner thighs, which were now trembling as slickness gathered between them.

"Bigger doesn't mean stronger," she grunted before lifting her free hand, intending to punch every tooth out of his mouth.

He caught her balled fist in his palm as if she'd aimed for it. Sputtering, she cursed and struggled against him as he lifted that arm beside her other one. Securing her wrists tight in one hand above her head, he closed the remaining distance between them, fully aligning their bodies. The contact drove her insane with lust, and she looked away, unable to meet his eyes.

He cupped her chin and forced her to meet his gaze.

The urge to lodge her knee in his balls roared, and recognition lit his brown irises. Full lips curled into a sexy grin as his warm breath skated across her cheek. "Don't do it," he murmured. "I desperately need that part of my anatomy."

"Not around me," she said. "I'm not Dani."

Dark eyes roved over her face, contemplative and hesitant. "Using Dani as an excuse isn't going to work anymore," he finally said. "My feelings for her were a coping mechanism. I know you understand that somewhere in that infuriatingly hard head." Sliding his fingers to her temple, he gently tapped. "They weren't real—"

"Of course they were real," she said, frustrated at the incessant pounding of the treacherous organ in her chest. "Everyone loves Dani. She's gorgeous, brilliant, funny. It makes perfect sense."

Sliding his hand from her temple to her neck, he placed his palm over her pulsing vein. The pad of his thumb caressed the sensitive skin as he spoke. "Dani is easy to love, but that's a completely separate topic."

Annoyance—and a hefty dose of pain—sliced through her, and she squirmed against him, trying to wrench her wrists from his death grip above her head. "Let me go!"

"Wait," he said with a frustrated shake of his head.

"So you can tell me how much you love my sister? That's fucking weird, Dom."

Thick nostrils flared as his eyes darted between hers. "Jesus, woman, you're infuriating."

"*I'm* infuriating? You just told me you loved my sister while you're holding me in some sexual death grip against the wall!"

Huffing a laugh, he shook his head, appearing to try and rid it from the strange conversation. "I said Dani is easy to love because it's true. She isn't as stubborn and immobile as some other women I know." Arching a brow, he shot her a heated glare.

"If I wasn't stubborn, we'd all be dead. It's what makes me a good fighter."

"True." Ever so slowly, he leaned forward, his lips only a hairsbreadth from hers.

Ari gasped, mortified her knees were close to buckling. His warm breath enveloped her and she fought the urge to close her eyes and lean into his massive frame.

"You're stubborn...and fierce...and gorgeous..." His lips brushed hers as he spoke the words. "And you're not easy, Ari. You require effort and dedication, and I was lazy with you for far too long."

"I don't want your effort—"

"Liar," he whispered, resting his forehead against hers. The skin of her face tingled in every spot his skin pressed against hers. "I think you want me as much as I want you."

She shook her head, terrified of the intense feelings clamoring to breach the surface. "No, I don't."

He gazed into her as their breaths mingled. "You're not easy to love, sweetheart," he said, the words surrounding her and causing her to shiver. "But I'm tired of easy. I took that route for a long fucking time because I was broken. I didn't see what was right in front of me."

Scattered breaths exited her lips as arousal ripped through every cell in her body, burning her from the inside out. "I won't be a substitute for Dani, and I don't do romantic relationships," she said, lowering her gaze, unable to meet his eyes. "I'm not cut out for any of that shit—"

"Shut up," he interrupted, squeezing the juncture of her neck and shoulder. "Just shut up and feel, Ari."

Emotion swamped her as she felt the sting of tears. How long had she loved this man who was in love with someone else? Her own *sister*, although she understood why he'd chosen Dani. Men always chose other women above her. It was a lesson she'd learned countless times and was too exhausted to repeat.

But now he was holding her, whispering about love and a thousand other things her brain couldn't process. Mortified, her heart pounded as tears clouded her gaze.

"*Shhh*," he whispered, empathy lacing the hushed command. "I'm sorry I fucked this up so badly, but that ends today."

Pushing the emotion away, she capitulated, trying to regain some control. "If you want to fuck, just say so. It's been a while, and I can see the benefit of blowing off some steam—"

"No," he interjected, covering her lips with his thumb—the dominant action so sexy her legs almost gave out. "I'm going to *make love* to you, Arianna. You deserve that, and I'm going to give it to you."

Releasing her wrists, he snaked his arm around her waist and dragged her against his body.

Arianna held her hands high, unsure what to do. If he fucked her with emotion instead of just raw sexual energy, it would be over for her. She'd probably fall so much deeper in love with him she'd be unable to fight it. And fighting was all she knew.

"I don't make love," she rasped, "I fuck. So if you want to fuck me, do it. Otherwise, I'm not interested."

Those sexy lips curved into a sensual grin that damn near set her panties on fire. Squirming, she acknowledged she'd have to lower her arms soon since they were trembling like the rest of her traitorous body.

"Challenge accepted. Put your arms around my neck, sweetheart."

"Don't call me that."

His lips twitched. "Put your arms around my neck, Arianna."

Lulled by his soft command, she lowered her arms and clenched them around his neck.

"*Good girl.*"

Shivering at the silken words, her body vibrated when a mischievous glint entered his eyes.

"You like being praised," he murmured, pressing every inch of his body against hers. "I'll remember that. As long as you're good, I'll reward you—"

"You talk too much," she hissed, spearing her nails into his neck. He uttered a curse before she inhaled it from his lips, closing her mouth over his.

A deep groan rumbled in his chest, and Arianna felt it to her core as he lowered his hands and cupped her ass in both palms. Lifting her, he pushed her back into the wall as he surged his erection into her core. Her legs encircled his waist, clutching for dear life, trusting him to hold her since her body was out of control with rampant desire.

Squeezing him with every ounce of strength she possessed, she thrust her tongue in his mouth, aching to taste every inch of the man she'd silently loved since the day they met.

Chapter 16

Dominic devoured Arianna's lips, overcome with her taste and smell. Her tongue flitted over his, smoother than the finest silk, and her legs squeezed him so tightly he thought his hips might break. Who cared when his tongue was buried inside her hot mouth and his cock was cradled in her sweet warmth? Aching to lose their clothes, he lifted her from the wall, never breaking their kiss as he carried her to the bedroom.

Once his knees brushed the mattress, he felt her pull away as she anticipated him releasing her. "Not yet," he murmured into the wet heat of her mouth. "Keep kissing me."

She rewarded him with a lusty purr, the sound crawling down his throat and driving him mad. Clutching her for dear life, he threw himself into the kiss of the century, sliding his tongue over every crevice of hers before retreating. Placing a soft peck on her lips, he expelled a deep, satisfied breath as he waited for her to open her eyes.

Lids laced with long, black eyelashes slowly rose, the irises behind them glassy with desire and a slight bit of doubt. Dominic's insides swirled with lust and emotion as he ran a hand over the baby hairs growing over the shaved side of her head. "Goddamnit, you're beautiful."

She stared back, weary and breathless as she seemed to ponder.

"I don't have protection," he said, gazing deep into her eyes. "But I haven't been with anyone in years."

"Neither have I," she said, "but I can still get pregnant."

A surge of possessive satisfaction zipped down his spine at the thought. It was misplaced and light-years from where they were now, but Dominic couldn't deny its vehemence. The thought of her strong, gorgeous body full with his child sent a shot of renewed arousal to his dick, and he undulated against her core, pleased at her resulting gasp.

"I'll pull out, but only if you say it's okay."

Her eyes darted between his as she contemplated. Inhaling a deep breath, she nodded. "Okay."

Joy surged through him so intensely he realized he needed to set her down before he damn near collapsed. Resting one knee on the bed, he gently lowered her, her back pressing against the bedspread as she stared up at him.

Her hair was braided into a thick strand, and he drew it across the bed, fanning it from her head so she could relax. Stunning eyes with those thick-as-hell lashes stared back at him above her angular nose and swollen lips. God, how could he have wasted time on Dani when *she* had been in front of him? He really was a goddamn idiot.

"You're staring," she whispered, eyebrows drawing together.

"It's all I'm capable of at the moment," he murmured, tracing her soft skin from the corner of her eye to those luscious lips. "I've been fantasizing about this moment for a while."

The tip of her tongue darted out, and she slowly ran it across her lips, wetting the luscious flesh. "What did I do to you in these fantasies?"

Groaning, he wedged her legs open with his, craving her core against his cock. "You used those pretty lips to suck me dry, Ari."

Red splotches marred her cheeks, making her look adorable as he loomed above her. He'd rarely seen her like this—relaxed and open—and it set something free deep within.

"And you opened up to me and let me fuck you until we both screamed." Undulating against her, he reveled in her quick inhale.

"So stop stalling and let's do it."

Chuckling, he nudged her nose with his. "Yes, ma'am."

Rising, he tore at his clothes, dragging them off as she reached for hers.

"Wait," he commanded, tossing his shirt on the floor and kicking off his boots. "I want to undress you."

She stilled, those brilliant eyes glowing with desire and a slight hesitation, before sliding her hands over her head. She was spread in front of him like a gorgeous present he couldn't wait to unwrap.

Once he was naked, he strode toward her, staring deep into her eyes as he tugged off her pants before gripping the hem of her shirt. Lifting from the bed, she allowed him to pull it off and throw it aside before he traced the hem of her bra.

"No lacy lingerie here," she murmured, gauging his reaction from half-lidded eyes. "I hate fancy shit like that—"

"You're fucking perfect," he interrupted, unable to stop himself from running his palm over her breasts, covered by the black fabric. "I'm going to tell you every goddamn hour of every goddamn day until you believe me, Ari."

A joyful laugh escaped her throat, causing him to smile. "Wow. You like the functional underwear. I'm not sure what to do with that."

Stretching over her, he softly pressed his lips to hers. "I like anything you wear…"

Her lips caught his, capturing the words as he groaned. Undulating his hips, he pressed into her core, feeling the damp heat. Tremors shook his frame as he recognized the inevitable. He'd promised himself he'd go slow the first time—that he'd savor every second—but now that he was stretched above her, he admitted the lie.

"I need to fuck you," he rasped in her mouth. "I don't think I can go slow—"

"Take off my bra," she whispered, her breathing heavy as he removed the garment. His fingers shook as he slid her underwear down her long legs before tossing them away. Inhaling a deep breath, he froze, needing to bask in the vision before him for just a moment.

Slightly curved hips led to thick thighs and strong calves, the skin covered with a sheen of dark hair he craved against his palms. Dying to touch her, he rested his fingertips on her inner thighs, pressing her legs open and baring her glistening pussy.

"Not a lot of time for self-care," she murmured, opening beneath him. "I don't think I've shaved my legs—or anywhere else besides my head—in years."

"You're stunning," he whispered, running his palms over the soft skin of her legs, reveling in the slight luster of silken hair that felt so good against his skin. Continuing to caress her, he let his eyes travel over her pert breasts, the nipples tight and pointed in the exposed air. The areolas were dark—so much darker than the surrounding skin—and the contrast set him on fire.

Dominic knew Arianna didn't open herself to many men. The fact she would open herself to him shattered something deep inside his soul as he stared at her. Determined to thank her properly, he glided his hand up her thigh, shivering at her quiet moan as his fingers rested against her wet opening.

"Ari," he whispered, dragging his finger through her slickness. "You're dripping for me, aren't you?"

She gave a slight nod, her braid moving against the comforter as she gazed at him.

Placing two fingers at her core, he stared into those brilliant eyes before gently easing inside and coating them with her essence. White teeth toyed with her bottom lip as she rose to meet his fingers.

"*Good girl*," he growled, loving how she shivered at his praise. She certainly didn't need praise in other areas, but he understood that strong women sometimes liked to be dominated in bed. It provided a brief moment they could relinquish the need to be resilient and could just focus on *feeling*.

"I see you," he almost whispered, lifting the fingers now coated with her slick and touching them to her nipple. "I'm going to take care of you." Gazing into her eyes, he spread her wet arousal around the turgid nipple.

"*Oh god...*" she moaned, head thrown back as the pulse pounded in her neck. "*Dom...*"

"Don't look away," he softly commanded, lowering his fingers to press inside her again. Circling her tight vise, he gathered more wetness before lifting to coat her other nipple. "I want to look into those pretty eyes when I kiss you..." Spreading the slick over the tight bud, his cock jerked when she retrained her gaze on his. "And when I fuck you."

The curves of her breasts trembled slightly beneath the now-glistening nipples, and Dominic struggled to breathe. Sliding his hand beneath her knee, he wrapped her leg around his waist, the tip of his cock searching for her wet, pulsing core. Hissing at the contact, he lowered his head, eyes locked with hers as his mouth hovered above her nipple. Gazing into her soul, he closed his mouth around the tight bud as he began to push inside her.

Her resulting whimper sent every remaining drop of blood to his cock as he pushed deeper, lapping her nipple with his tongue as he inched inside her. Tight wetness met his steel, clenching his most sensitive place as he sucked her between his lips. Desperate for a stronghold, he reached for her, sliding his fingers into the hair beneath her braid and clutching for dear life.

"That's right, Ari," he rasped against her nipple, slowly dragging his sensitive flesh through her wet core before kissing a trail to her other breast. "You're mine now."

"I'm not anyone's—" she choked before gasping when he closed his teeth around her nipple, gently biting.

"So goddamn difficult," he grunted, increasing the pace of his hips as he licked the turgid bud to ease the sting. "It's one of my favorite things about you."

Her lips fell open with a soft cry as he increased the pace, his cock now sliding back and forth through her warmth as he struggled to hold on. Determined to please her first, he sucked her nipple deep, giving it one last, firm pull before lifting and withdrawing.

"Dom?" she asked, confusion lacing her expression beneath her flushed cheeks.

Unable to speak, he encircled her wrist and drew her toward the edge of the bed. Too impatient to gently instruct her, he pulled her to her feet before placing his hands on her hips and turning her to face the bed. "Get on your knees," he commanded.

"What the—?"

Grasping her braid, he gently tugged her head, reveling in her arousal-laden gasp. Nudging her with his hips, he pressed his lips against the shell of her ear. "Get on your fucking knees, Ari."

Arduous breaths exited her lungs as she followed his command, her submission sending a surge of joy through his veins so intense he almost whimpered. Pressing his chest to her back, he urged her to rest her head on his shoulder by tenderly tugging her braid. Once she was flush against him, he pressed his cock between the firm globes of her ass.

Resting his forehead to her temple, he spoke softly in her ear. "Open your legs."

She complied, widening her knees on the bed as he glided his fingers across her hip, reveling as the skin quivered beneath before reaching her mound. Sliding his fingers between her wet folds, he searched for her tight sensitive nub.

He began to rub her clit in concentric circles as his warm breath fanned over her ear. "If you think I'm going to get off without you coming first, you don't know me, Ari. All I want is to make you feel good." Searching for her opening with the head of his cock, he groaned when he found her slick core. Pressing against her as he stimulated her clit, he began to push inside from behind as she purred.

"That's it," he hissed in her ear, determined to make her scream before he sought his release. "Now, I need you to come for me."

"*Dom...*" she cried, lips glistening from the ardent swipes of her tongue as she undulated into his fingers, her body taking the sharp jabs of his cock as if she were made for him.

"So sweet and wet..." he crooned, his fingers moving furiously over her clit as he fucked her from behind.

Scoffing, she pressed her face against his neck. "I'm *not* sweet."

Chuckling, he bit her earlobe, pleased when she mewled in approval. "Your pussy is the sweetest thing I've ever felt around my cock. Now be a good girl and come around me. I want to feel you gush all over my fingers. Do you hear me?"

"I can't...*oh god,*" she rasped, reaching behind to grasp his hips as they hammered against her. Uncontrollable tremors shook her frame, and he knew she was close.

Short, pointed fingernails speared into the flesh of his ass as her body bowed and she screamed his name. Overcome with joy, he pressed his cheek into her temple, kissing her as he murmured words of praise and desire. The muscles of her core spasmed, milking him as he thrust between the wet, plushy folds. Gratified he could bring her such pleasure, he held her tight, cupping her mound as her body quaked and vibrated against his.

Needing more, he gently pushed her to the bed, pressing her chest to the soft mattress before securing her hips with both hands. Lifting her to her knees, he clenched tight as he began to pummel her with his hard cock.

"Jesus, you're still coming around me..." he groaned, tossing his head back and closing his eyes against the onslaught of pleasure. The sounds of their wet flesh slapping together rang in his ears as he fought to hold off his release. Gritting his teeth, he realized the pleasure was too much to bear. Giving in to the overwhelming bliss, he fucked her as his release gathered at the base of his cock.

Screaming unintelligible words, he gripped her shoulder, holding firm as he pumped inside her, feeling the jets of release form before he pulled out and began to come.

He covered her body, wrapping his arms around her as he emptied everything against her smooth back. "So fucking good," he groaned, burying his face in her neck as jets of release drenched her ravaged body.

They quaked and shuddered, lost to desire as they clung to each other, uttering indecipherable words while pleasure threatened to drown them. Eventually, Dominic lost the ability to move, the orgasm draining every ounce of energy from his frame. Unable to support himself, he collapsed further, thankful she was strong and could support his weight.

Overwhelmed by her scent and the way she instinctively curled into him, he nuzzled her neck and slid his arm between her breasts, drawing her closer.

"Ari," he whispered, wrapping his leg around her thigh, curving her into his body as he haphazardly spooned her atop the soft mattress. "Good grief," he mumbled, trailing soft kisses over the back of her neck, thrilled when tiny bumps rose against his lips. "Is that what it's going to be like every time I fuck you?" Squeezing her, he aimed to merge every cell in his body to hers. "I'm not sure I'll survive."

Wriggling her ass into his sated body, she chuckled. "Who says this wasn't just a one-time thing?"

"I say," was his quick response before he nipped her earlobe, causing her to quiver in his arms. "I can't live without fucking you again. It's impossible."

A contented purr exited her lips as she relaxed against him. "You lived this long and did just fine..." Yawning, she snuggled deeper into his embrace.

"I was a fool," he murmured, kissing the shell of her ear. Reaching over, he grabbed some tissues from the dresser and wiped the skin between them, cleaning his release. Tossing them away, he snuggled against her again, acknowledging how perfectly she fit into the grooves of his body. "Never again. Do you hear me? I'll apologize for eternity if you let me keep fucking you."

A soft laugh rumbled from her throat. "We'll see. For now, I need sleep. Sun will be up soon so we can jog..."

Inhaling her scent, he burrowed deeper into her as his eyelids grew heavy. "Or we could sleep past sunrise like two normal people who just had amazing sex and forget the world is a dumpster fire."

Her resulting grunt was the perfect response, causing him to grin as he held her. Part of him wanted to push her—to make her admit what they'd done was light-years from a quick, meaningless fuck. She'd sucked every piece of his soul into her gorgeous body, and he never wanted it back. Could she open herself up enough to admit her feelings?

Hesitant to rile her when she was so warm and pliant against him, Dominic decided to table a serious discussion until after they'd made love a few more times. One day soon, he would gather the courage to tell her he was all in. That the bullet he'd taken in the lab had reset something in his brain...in his *heart*...and he was ready to take the incredible risk of trying to love again.

That *she* was worth the risk.

Gently stroking her shoulder, he nuzzled the tender skin behind her ear until her muscles grew limp. Once he was surrounded by her soft snores, he closed his eyes and gave in to the magnificent pleasure of falling asleep with Arianna curled against his body.

Chapter 17

Arianna awoke to the delicious smell of Dominic *everywhere*. That evergreen scent that haunted her dreams surrounded her as she rubbed her leg over his hairy thigh. Sometime during the night, they'd shifted in the bed to lay properly on the pillows. Lifting her lids, the first thing Arianna saw was the scar on his neck, the skin still slightly puffed under the healing wound.

Aching to touch him—to confirm he was okay—she touched the scar with the pad of her finger and began to gently trace it. Dominic inhaled a deep breath before turning his head on the pillow to face her.

She gazed into his eyes as she tenderly ran her finger over the laceration. "I didn't want you to draw the soldiers out last night because I was scared. I can't see you hurt again, Dom."

His lips formed a tender smile as he cupped her cheek. "I figured that was why you disobeyed my order."

Arianna rolled her eyes. "I don't care how good of a lay you are, I don't take orders from anyone."

Arching his eyebrow, he smirked. "So you're saying I'm the best you've ever had?"

"*Pfft*. Get over yourself. You're certainly the best I've had in a while though. I haven't had any interest in men in a long time."

Dominic's thumb caressed her cheek, back and forth in slow, fluid motions that made her want to curl into him and languish all day.

"But that's not going to get you out of training. We need to run at least ten miles and then grab some breakfast from Deandra. Hopefully, she'll have an update on the tailor."

They'd stopped in the deli yesterday to ask for the best place to shop for formal clothes that was inconspicuous. Deandra informed them she knew a friend who was a dry cleaner and tailor who had several tuxedos and gowns that had never been picked up. Deandra had promised to speak to him and see if he was open to lending them.

"Let's start the day off properly before we get back to saving the world," Dominic said, lowering his hand and cupping her ass. He drew her against his body, his skin warm as his cock searched for her.

"The more we do this, the more chances we take, Dom." Even as she heard the warning in her voice, she opened herself to him, allowing him inside. Biting her lip, she winced at the soreness down below.

"You okay?" he asked, halting as concern entered his deep brown eyes.

"Yeah," she whispered, pushing into him. "Just sore."

"I can stop—"

She covered his lips. "Not on your fucking life."

The smooth slide of his cock sent a warm glow throughout her body. Their cheeks rested on the pillows as they gazed into each other's eyes, the moment more intimate than she'd anticipated.

Part of her wanted to retreat behind her shell and protect all the parts she'd bared to him. But in a deep corner of her heart, she held hope that maybe, just maybe, things could be different with Dominic.

She palmed his jaw, her eyes roving over the scar that ran from the corner of one eye, over his nose, to the far side of his lips.

"It's not pretty," he muttered, fucking her in firm strokes as his fingers dug into her ass.

"I don't need pretty," she whispered, undulating into his deft movements. "I just need you to keep fucking me."

His resulting groan reverberated through every cell as he pressed her back on the mattress. Sliding over her, he loomed above as he increased the pace.

"You take me so well, Arianna," he crooned, causing her eyes to roll back in her head with pleasure. God, she could listen to that deep voice as he claimed her every hour of every damn day.

"Dom..."

"Take me deep, sweetheart," he rasped, hitting the spot inside that had been neglected for so long. Arianna's head tilted back on the pillow, and he placed wet kisses along her neck as they reached the crescendo.

With a groan, he pulled from her body, emptying on her stomach as she launched into her climax. Her muscles shook and quaked as he released above her before collapsing atop her quivering body.

Dominic's breath heated her neck as he exhaled, his face buried against her skin.

"We need to buy some condoms," she said, trailing her fingers over his back as he nearly crushed her. Another woman might have complained, but Arianna was tough and loved his weight atop her.

"I like feeling you bare around me," he said against her neck.

"Yes, but barebacking results in babies, and that's not in my plan at the moment."

Lifting his head, he studied her. "It's in your plan after Dani finishes the antidote and we defeat Cromwell."

"Sure, in a perfect world. But who knows when that will happen?"

Disappointment laced his features as he frowned. "Fine. But we're coming back to this discussion when we're both ready."

The corner of Arianna's mouth ticked up. "I told you. I've already got a plan. A turkey baster and a secluded cabin. That's all I need."

The challenge that lit his eyes was sexy as hell. "We'll see." Pecking her lips, he pushed up and slid into a sitting position. "You want to shower before we jog? We made a mess."

"Yeah." Sitting up, she ran her hand over her disheveled braid. "Give me five minutes, then you can jump in after."

"I can jump in with you," he said, his lips curling into a sexy grin.

Chuckling, she shook her head and rose. "If you do that, we'll never go running. And we both need the exercise."

Before he could argue, she slipped into the nearby bathroom and shut the door.

As she showered under the lukewarm spray—which was all they got at the shitty motel—she smiled as she ran the cloth over her sore entrance. Making love to Dominic had been even more pleasurable than she'd imagined. The way he demanded her submission, somehow knowing she craved it, had set something free inside her.

After rinsing off the suds, she stepped onto the mat and dried her skin, grinning at her reflection in the foggy mirror like a lovesick dope. No matter how much she denied it, she knew the truth: now that she'd had sex with Dominic, there was no turning back.

Covering her heart, she gazed into her eyes in the mirror.

"Careful, Arianna," she whispered.

The thrum of her ragged heartbeat was the only response to her quiet plea.

CHAPTER 18

After a brisk jog and another quick shower—alone, much to Dominic's chagrin—they returned to Matt and Susan's apartment. Dominic thought Arianna's head might explode when Matt opened the door and told her he hadn't yet obtained Tristan's address.

"I told you the timeline was firm, Matt," Arianna said, a muscle ticking in her jaw. "We're here to find my sister, and I know you have the resources to do it."

"Matt's shift starts in two hours, and he's going to do some digging while he's with Luthor," Susan said, appearing behind Matt and sliding a supportive hand over his shoulder. "Selena has lunch with Luthor and his wife, Grace, today. Tristan used to be married to Grace, and we think she might know where he lives."

Arianna's head whipped around. "Tristan was married to Luthor's *wife*?" Her eyes almost bugged out of her head. "That would've been good to know."

"Perhaps a possible motive for his desire to murder him," Dominic said, arching a brow.

Arianna grunted before facing Matt again. "Okay, I won't shoot you in the balls since you gave me that info. What about the birthday party?" she asked Susan.

"You're all set," she said, appearing pleased with herself. "You're on the list under the names David and Amy Ratched."

Arianna shot her a scathing glare. "Am I supposed to infer I'm 'Nurse Ratched' in this scenario?"

Dominic pursed his lips to stifle his laugh. It was pretty funny and an accurate representation of how Susan probably saw Arianna.

"Oh, that was just coincidence." She innocently batted her eyelashes.

"I bet." Arianna's tone dripped with sarcasm. "Do we need tickets or anything?"

"Nope. Just show up and give them your names. You're going to need these." She thrust out a pair of ID cards with their fake names on them.

"Well, damn," Arianna said, inspecting them before handing them to Dom. "You came through, Susan. Thank you."

Dominic stuck the two plastic cards in the side pocket of his pack, zipping it closed to keep them safe.

"I'll be home after lunch today to get ready for Luthor's birthday party," Matt said. "Selena doesn't need me until six p.m. when she's ready to head over. I can tell you if I found out anything over lunch."

"Just tell me at the party," Arianna said. "I'll find a way for us to speak privately."

"Will do."

"Okay, I've got to clean this one up and find a dress to wear." She pointed at Dominic while grimacing in distaste. "I don't think I've worn a dress in years. Gross, but necessary. Will I see you both there tonight?"

"I won't be there since Mattie's working," Susan said, hugging his arm as she nuzzled into his side. "But I hope you find Raquel, Arianna. I really do."

"Thanks. See you there, Matt." With a small salute, she turned and headed down the stairs. Dominic said his goodbyes and trailed after her, ready to try on some unclaimed tuxedos.

Two hours later, Dominic stood in front of the full-length mirror in the back of a dingy dry cleaner business that had seen better days. Deandra had come through, and she'd left Ron to man the deli while she'd accompanied them to the tailor two blocks away.

"Come on out, Arianna," Deandra called, her tone impatient. "This is the third dress you've tried on, and I'm sure it's fine."

Arianna's annoyed huff sounded from her dressing room as Dominic threaded the final button on his collar.

"I think this tux works," he said, pulling back the curtain and stepping out of the small makeshift dressing room. "What do you think?"

"Looks nice," Deandra said, approaching him. "Tommy, do you have a bowtie?"

The owner, an older man who appeared to be at least seventy, with snow-white hair and bushy eyebrows, nodded. He scuffled to the front and returned with a black bow tie. Deandra threaded it through Dominic's white collared shirt and began to tie it.

"Do you know how to do this?" she asked.

"Not really, but I'm a fast learner."

She smiled and tied the black material as she talked. "Over this way and through the loop here. See?" Tightening the bow, she beamed. "Perfect. Now, you try."

Dominic untied the material and tried to follow her instructions. Gazing in the mirror affixed to the wall, he stuck his tongue between his teeth as he worked.

"Excellent job," Deandra said, patting the bow when he was finished. "You'll do just fine tonight."

Dominic studied the woman's deep brown eyes. "You're going out of your way to help two strangers. I find myself wondering why."

Sadness crept into her expression. "We lost our son to EverLife. He was twenty-three and had his whole life ahead of him. Arianna didn't divulge much about your mission, but she told me her sister is working for Luthor. My assumption is that you're going to the fancy party tonight to find her and convince her to leave Washington, DC. Am I wrong?"

Dominic pursed his lips as he studied the wily woman. "No, but I gather you're rarely wrong, Deandra."

She emitted a good-natured scoff. "Tell that to my husband, infuriating man." Her eyes sparkled, offsetting her words. "And I also assume that once you rescue her sister, you'll regroup and return to the city to try and immobilize Cromwell."

"If I confirmed that, I'd have to kill you," he joked as the corner of his lips quirked.

Staring into Dominic's eyes, she spoke with clarity. "I hate Luthor Cromwell with a passion. I keep my ear to the ground in the hope a rebellion forms. I hear mumblings and have seen the graffiti, but nothing has come to fruition yet." Patting his chest, she lifted an eyebrow. "Maybe you and Arianna can change that."

"We'd love to know what you've heard," Dominic said. "Any information is valuable."

Deandra opened her mouth to reply at the same moment Arianna stepped out from the other dressing room. A sharp breath exited Dominic's lungs as his eyes raked over her body in the long, flowing red gown. "That's the one," he said, his mouth suddenly dry.

Arianna's eyes met his, the green flecks enhanced by the deep red color. It was simple, with a smattering of sparkles on the shoulder straps lowering to a V that showed off her cleavage. Noticing the flare of her hips, Dominic worked his jaw, attempting to regain his ability to speak.

"Down boy," Deandra teased, touching him under his chin and gently forcing his mouth closed. "I think your man likes it, Arianna."

"Not my man, but if it's passible, I'm happy." Stretching out her arms, she rotated in front of the mirror.

Dominic stepped toward her, his pulse pounding as he gently cupped both of her shoulders. "Holy shit. You look amazing."

"Okay, calm down," she said, but he saw the spark of pleasure in her eyes at his compliment. "You might have to help me get in and out of this thing later."

"Oh, I think he's counting on it," Deandra said, her eyes filled with mirth as she grinned.

Arianna chuckled and nodded. "Okay, we'll take it. Do we owe you anything for the clothes, Tommy?"

"No charge. Deandra's friends are always welcome to borrow my clothes," the owner said.

"Give him a gold bar," Arianna said softly to Dominic.

"Was already planning on it."

After the tuxedo and dress had been packed up, they began the short trip back to the deli.

"Deandra was going to tell me all the intel she knows about the rebellion," Dominic said as they trailed down the sidewalk.

"Was I?" she asked, shooting him a playful glare. "I don't know much, but Ron and I try our best to glean information where and when we can. Our customers talk a bit too loudly sometimes when they're in line waiting for Ron's sandwiches."

"We're grateful for anything you can tell us," Arianna said.

"We mostly hear people grumbling about Cromwell and how they detest his grip on the city," Deandra said, stopping in front of the deli. "The rich folks might like the status quo, but for the rest of us, it's not so grand." Rubbing her chin, she contemplated. "I honestly don't have much to tell. You already know the visible hints of the rebellion from the graffiti. But there is something..."

"Whatever it is, it might help," Arianna said.

Leaning forward, Deandra lowered her voice, as if she didn't want anyone else to hear, even though they were alone on the sidewalk. "Some of the conversations I've overheard speculate that the genesis of the rebellion is from *inside* Luthor's circle."

Arianna's eyebrows lifted. "Interesting. We know it's not Tristan," she said to Dominic. "Unless he was lying, which I wouldn't put past him."

"Tristan isn't in Luthor's *inner* circle," Deandra said. "He's still a paid employee, which Luthor considers beneath him."

Arianna's mouth fell open. "You know Tristan too? Is there anyone who doesn't know this guy?"

Chuckling, Deandra tilted her head. "Tristan Holder visits the deli every once in a while. He makes it his business to know what's going on in every part of the city. Sometimes, I tell him things I think he needs to hear."

"You would've made a fantastic spy, Deandra," Dominic said, admiration in his voice. "And still might depending on how things unfold."

"For you?" she asked good-naturedly. "I might consider it depending on the day." She winked. "Anyway, if I had to guess, I would imagine one of the other rich cronies might want to take Luthor down. I've heard several names tossed around, including George Luddington and James Stalworth."

"Both of whom were two of the wealthiest men in the world before it collapsed," Dominic said, recalling both men had been CEOs of huge companies and frequently appeared on the "Richest Men Alive" lists.

"And now the title of richest man has been relinquished to Luthor Cromwell. I'm not sure ol' George and James are too thrilled with that," Deandra said.

"Do you know of any specific plans?" Arianna asked.

"No. Some of their employees frequent the deli, and I overhear their conversations about how their bosses don't even bother to hide their disdain for Luthor. It might be worth investigating at your fancy party tonight."

"Absolutely. I'm sure both men will be in attendance. Rich assholes usually flock together, right?" Arianna asked.

Dominic shrugged. "Can't say I've known many rich assholes, but if they're in attendance, we'll surveil them. On another note, how functional is the Metro system in the city?"

Deandra wrinkled her nose. "Barely. Luthor had his tech team set up the trains to run automatically so they didn't need human operators. But they rarely run on time—if at all—and the stations are filled with addicts and homeless people."

"That means we should probably walk to the party," Arianna said. "It's warm today and shouldn't take more than two hours." Glancing at Deandra, she asked, "You don't happen to have any flats I can borrow, do you? My boots don't quite go with my dress, and flats are all I can manage if we walk."

"If you can wear an eight and a half, I do," she said with a nod.

"I'm a nine but close enough."

After procuring the flats from their apartment above the deli, Deandra walked them outside.

"We really appreciate your help, Deandra," Dominic said. "Thank you."

"You're welcome. Now, let me get back and help Ron. I'm already going to get a stern lecture for leaving him alone for an hour."

After saying their goodbyes, Dominic walked with Arianna to the pharmacy they'd spotted a few blocks from the motel. When they found the boxes of condoms hanging from the hooks in the narrow aisle, Arianna snatched one up and began heading to the register.

"Hey!" Dominic said, tugging her back. "You're not even going to buy the super-magnum ones? Are you trying to give me a complex?"

Arianna rolled her eyes at his teasing. "Don't flatter your-self."

Flashing her a grin, he pulled three more boxes from the hooks.

"Geez, Dom. We'll never use that many."

"Woman, I love your challenges." Leaning over, he gave a dramatic bow. "And I accept. We'll make use of every one of these suckers." Straightening, he shook one of the boxes at her.

She exhaled an exasperated breath, but Dominic caught the bare hint of a smile that tugged at her lips. "Fine. Buy them all. You can explain to Arthur where all his money went."

She strode toward the counter in that regal way that set his body on fire. After they purchased the condoms, they made their way back to the motel to get ready for the party.

"Should we break them in?" Dominic asked, waggling his eyebrows once they were in the hotel room.

Arianna chewed on her bottom lip. "I'm here for Raquel, Dom. I don't want to get distracted."

"We'll see Raquel in a few hours if all goes to plan." Closing the distance between them, he placed his fingers under her chin and tilted her head to look into her eyes. "And I can do a *lot* to your body in a few hours."

Those stunning eyes darted back and forth between his for a small eternity before she took pity on him. Her tongue darted out to bathe her lips and she finally whispered, "Prove it."

Dominic lurched for her, lifting her over his shoulder and carrying her to bed. Her high-pitched squeal was soon silenced by his lips as he endeavored to meet her challenge.

Chapter 19

Luthor Cromwell paced across the dark carpet that lined the conference room floor. His steps were measured as he circled the ornate mahogany table where Tristan sat alongside other members of Luthor's security team. Tristan wasn't always invited to these meetings since he was technically a mercenary, but Luthor was receiving reports about his small network of scientists, which included Raquel.

"How's our little botanist doing?" Luthor asked, stopping behind Tristan's chair and placing his hands over the leather headrest.

Tristan stared ahead, eyeing the men who sat across from him rather than looking up to meet Luthor's gaze. "Fine. She's usually out the door early and home by seven. She seems to take her work seriously and is an amenable houseguest."

Luthor uttered a thoughtful "Hmmm" before strolling back toward the head of the conference table. Lowering into the plushy leather seat, his eyes narrowed. "She doesn't mention her sister? Nor show any remorse about betraying her?"

"No. She's dedicated to your cause, Luthor. She hasn't mentioned Danica to me at all."

Luthor steepled his fingers and tapped them against his lips as he pondered. "Good. She's making excellent progress on a new antidote that will offer short-term relief before the addiction sets back in. It lessens the side effects, so I anticipate some of the remaining holdouts will try EverLife. It's important we get everyone in our new society on board. We can't have the majority of the population live extended lives while a small percentage experience normal lifespans."

Tristan scoffed, inwardly remarking that his comments seemed almost altruistic. As if he wanted something good for society instead of the destruction that came with each new person who succumbed to the addictive drug.

"Did you have more to add, Tristan?" Luthor asked, a warning in his tone.

"No, sir."

Leaning back, Luthor rotated slowly in the chair as he studied him. "Maybe I can finally get you on board with EverLife. It doesn't make any sense to die decades before your sister, especially since I know you love her so much."

Biting the inside of his cheek, Tristan fought not to scream. Since Jessica was vehemently addicted to EverLife, she traded sexual favors to Luthor for the drug and the watered-down antidote. Until he could find a solution, she needed to remain in Luthor's good graces to receive purer stashes that weren't filled with the toxic garbage in the antidote outside the walls.

Which meant Tristan needed to stay on Luthor's good side to protect her. What a clusterfuck.

"Not on my agenda for the moment. I'm still an old-school holdout who prefers a clean diet and exercise to stay young."

Luthor's eyebrows lifted. "For now."

Lowering his eyes to shield his hate, Tristan remained silent, hoping the bastard would move on to another topic.

"Where are we with the soldier serum, Dr. Ziegler?" Luthor asked.

The man at the far end of the table in the white lab coat cleared his throat. "I'll be ready to test on human subjects soon, sir. The tests on the mice are almost complete and very promising."

"Excellent." Resting his forearms on the table, Luthor spoke with gravity. "And the trackers?"

Tristan's ears perked as he reminded himself to remain impassive. What or *who* was Luthor going to track?

"The microchip prototype is almost complete," Dr. Ziegler said. "As you know, my counterpart, Dr. Rajmani, was an expert in microchip technology at Capital Tech. We should be able to implant the first hundred test subjects by the end of the month. After a few weeks of observation, I anticipate being able to implant them in everyone left in the city."

"And the factory near the university in Maryland has the capacity to make that many units?"

"Yes, sir," Dr. Ziegler said with a nod. "The high-capacity generators your men installed are top notch, and we have many engineers who've volunteered to work on the assembly in exchange for the antidote, whether for themselves, family members or both."

Luthor nodded as he tapped his chin. "Good. I want George Luddington and James Stalworth on the list of the first hundred people microchipped."

"They won't be happy about that, sir," Colonel McGrath said from his seat to Luthor's right. "They still employ a large number of people in the city and have influence over public sentiment. Most of our soldiers' spouses work for them in some capacity, and they're seen as benevolent employers inside the walls."

"I don't give a shit *how* they're seen," Luthor said, slapping his palm against the table. "This is *my* city and *my* government, and those two idiots are no more important than anyone else. They will be microchipped in the first wave. Are we clear?"

Dr. Ziegler's throat bobbed. "Yes."

With a firm nod, Luthor inserted his finger between his collar and his neck, loosening the fabric as the vein there pulsed with anger. "Once the trackers are ready, I want the homeless rounded up and purged from the city. All graffiti is to be cleaned, and anyone who speaks of or promotes rebellion will be exiled as well."

"Sir," Colonel McGrath said, straightening, "are you sure that punishment fits the crime? Some people still remember democracy and feel they have the right to protest—"

"Democracy died when people chose to take my drug to enhance their lives!" Luthor interrupted, rising to his feet and slicing his hand through the air. "I make their new lives possible. If they accept my leadership, they will have a prosperous life inside these walls. It's not too much to ask, is it?"

The men exchanged hooded glances as they remained silent.

"Is it?"

"No, sir," a deep voice chimed. "We are loyal to you, and this is your city. Rebels should be and will be exiled."

Tristan's nostrils flared as he listened to Zayne Danvers, Luthor's head of security.

"Thank you, Zayne," Luthor said, lowering to his seat. "Your loyalty is appreciated." Making eye contact with each of the members, he asked softly, "Do I have your loyalty too?"

"Yes, sir," they said in unison.

"Good. I'd hate to see Tracy suffer the side effects of EverLife withdrawal," he said to Colonel McGrath. "Your wife is such a lovely woman."

"Thank you, sir," the colonel replied, a muscle ticking in his jaw as he gritted the words.

Inhaling a breath, Luthor leaned back in the chair. "Dissention doesn't sow peace or prosperity. Only strong leadership and a firm hand will do in these situations. I'm glad we're all on the same page."

Glancing at the other men, Tristan wasn't so sure everyone was on board, but he'd learned to pick his battles. Now, in a room full of soldiers and security guards, wasn't the time to make waves.

His fingers tightened on the arm rests as he imagined tightening them around the evil leader's throat instead. One day soon, the day would come to overthrow the madman, and Tristan would be ready. If there was one thing he'd learned since the world collapsed, it was that patience was an asset.

One day, in the not-so-distant future, an opportunity would present itself to take down Luthor Cromwell.

And that day would be one Tristan relished for all the days that followed in their godforsaken world.

Chapter 20

S everal hours later, Dominic's fingers maneuvered the bow tie as he waited for Arianna to exit the bedroom. When she appeared, he turned to face her, noting she'd twirled her hair into some sort of fancy bun at the side of her neck.

"Didn't think the braid was elegant enough," she said, pointing to the bun. "Does it look okay?"

Dominic closed the distance between them, unable to stop himself from touching her. "It looks gorgeous. You clean up pretty well, Lawson."

Laughing, she pointed to her face. "I think I'm still flushed from our afternoon activities. The natural glow works wonders."

They'd made love twice before collapsing and taking a short nap. Feeling invigorated after the great sex and a lukewarm shower, he squeezed her shoulders. "Need me to button or zip anything?"

"No, but you could put the necklace on for me?" She held it up in her palm, and Dominic took it before she turned around. His thick fingers fumbled with the clasp of the necklace Deandra had insisted on loaning her along with the shoes, and he eventually latched it. She turned to face him and pointed at her flat dress shoes.

"These aren't really my style, but I'm not in this to win any beauty contests."

"They look fine and the dress is stunning."

"I'm worried we won't have guns," she said, eyeing their weapons on the table. "But we can't take the chance since they'll definitely frisk us before we get anywhere near Cromwell."

"We're both skilled at combat and evasion. If we need to fight or run, we'll do it." Lifting a finger, he spoke in a low, resolved tone. "We need to work together and communicate. If I give you an order, don't question it."

Her silken eyebrow arched. "And if I give you an order?"

"I'll follow it," he said without hesitation.

Her throat bobbed as she studied him. "Okay. Remember, the main goal is to approach Raquel and figure out where her head's at so we can get her out of here. If we can also discover intel on the rebellion, even better."

Dominic gave a firm nod. "If we get separated, we'll need a meeting point. Let's identify that as soon as we get there and then we'll proceed."

With the plan set, they gathered up the IDs, and Dominic slid the cardigan they'd procured from Tommy over Arianna's bare arms. The walk would take them down Rhode Island Avenue, around Logan Circle, and eventually to the downtown rooftop restaurant where Luthor's party was being held.

Once they were on their way, Arianna was quiet as they walked.

"You okay?"

"Yeah, I'm just thinking about Raquel." Tiny lines of worry appeared between her eyes. "I've got to convince her to come with us. I'm worried she won't come willingly."

"There's no use in speculating until we get there," he said.

She nodded, the gesture morose in the waning sunlight. Reaching over, he clasped her hand.

Her eyebrows lifted as she spared him a glance. "I don't hold hands, Dom."

"Okay."

She responded with an exasperated little huff but didn't pull away.

Moments later, she laced her fingers with his.

Feeling his lips curve into a satisfied grin, he held tight as they made their way downtown.

As they neared the restaurant, Arianna noticed the streets evolved from dirty to clean to pristine. The blocks that surrounded downtown were meticulously maintained, and there were no homeless encampments in sight.

"Luthor must keep this part of town spotless to maintain the illusion for his rich cronies," Arianna said.

"People can only live under illusion for so long though" was Dominic's terse response.

Inwardly acknowledging that truth, she slid her hand over Dominic's forearm as they approached a red awning that read Celine's. "There's an alley a block away," she said, gesturing with her head.

Dominic craned his neck. "That works as a meeting point. We need to identify one inside as well."

"Somewhere near the door, preferably," she agreed. Dominic opened the building glass door for her, and they were met with four security guards in black suits—three men and one woman.

"Names, please."

"Amy and David Ratched," Arianna said, smiling politely.

The man looked over his clipboard before pointing to their names. "Welcome, Mr. and Mrs. Ratched. May I see your IDs?"

Once the IDs had been looked over, one of the guards gestured toward the metal detector. "Please, ma'am."

Arianna walked through slowly, followed by Dominic, who was pulled aside by one of the men.

"Sir, I just need to do a quick check for weapons. Lily will check you, ma'am."

The female security guard did a quick but thorough check of Arianna while Dominic received a similar pat down.

"Sending up one male and one female," the guard with the clipboard said into his smartwatch. Lily led them to the elevator and pushed the P before backing out. "Have a good time," she said with a wave.

They whooshed to the top as Arianna took a breath to steady herself. She hadn't seen Raquel since her terrible betrayal, and several emotions whirled within. Anger for her sister's actions. Concern for her well-being. Frustration she was working for Cromwell.

"We'll get her out of here," Dominic said, reading her thoughts in the way he was increasingly becoming excellent at. "Don't lose your temper with her."

"Who, me?" she asked sardonically as the doors slid open.

Dominic smirked as they exited the elevator. A large ballroom expanded in front of them, decorated with a multitude of blue and white balloon bundles along the walls. Music pumped from a DJ booth on the far side of the room, and the wooden dance floor glowed under the multicolored disco ball.

"Can I take your sweater, ma'am?"

Arianna's eyes darted to the coat room as she shook her head. "I'll keep it, thanks." She whispered to Dominic out of the corner of her mouth, "Coat room for the indoor meet-up spot."

"Confirmed."

They scanned the room before slowly trailing along the carpeted floor that circled the smooth dance floor. Lights pulsed from the disco ball as a smattering of people danced. Arianna's eyes darted across the dim room as she searched for Raquel.

"Anything?" she asked.

"Not yet."

They approached the bar that flanked the wall to the left in an attempt to appear as normal patrons.

"Scotch neat. Macallan 14 if you have it. And a vodka soda for my wife."

Arianna shot him a droll look as the bartender scampered away to make their drinks. "He scores a few times and thinks he can order for me," she muttered.

"I know you like vodka," he said, sliding his arm around her waist. "And I also liked watching your cheeks flush when I called you my wife."

"From anger," she retorted, but her tone also held a teasing note.

"Or wishful thinking." He winked.

"I'm not really into this side of you," she said, scrunching her features and waving her hand up and down his chest. "Leave the funny quips to Maverick. You suck at them."

Leaning forward, he touched his lips to the shell of her ear. "If you want me to call you my wife again, just ask nicely."

She elbowed him in the side, half-annoyed and half-elated when he responded with a chuckle. Very few people understood her sarcastic, broody nature, and most people bristled at it. Not Dominic. He'd never been intimidated by her. Not once. Wondering if that was something to be celebrated or chagrined, she took a sip of the drink the bartender placed in front of her.

Turning, she faced the large room and squinted as she assessed. "I guess Raquel's not here yet. The room's about a third full, but we're on time. People arrive fashionably late to these things, right?"

"I guess. Want to assess the terrace before it gets too full?"

Nodding, Arianna followed him outside into the rapidly cooling city air. There were a few people scattered on the terrace, which was lined with several small couches. Dominic headed toward the edge and looked over, whistling as he observed the street below.

"So different than when I used to live here. It's technically still a city, but the hustle and bustle is gone. It's a shell of what it once was."

Setting her glass on the ledge, she rested her forearms atop the cold stone and peered down. "The world will never be the same. It's kind of sad."

"If we're lucky, maybe we can eventually fashion it into something better than it ever was."

Facing him, she leaned against the wall. "Such an optimist. How do you still have hope? Sometimes, I wonder if we're wasting our time trying to fix everything."

"You can find hope in small corners of the world if you choose to look." Extending his hand, he held up his palm. "Dance with me."

"We can barely hear the music."

"I don't need music to move with you, Arianna." He hooked his upturned fingers.

Sighing, she placed her hand in his. "This is stupid—"

He drew her into his arms, away from the ledge, as their drinks sat there, forgotten. Her arm slid around his neck as he clasped her hand, holding it at shoulder height as they began to sway.

"I've always wanted to make it up to you," he said softly as their bodies moved in a slow rhythm.

Her eyebrows drew together.

"The first time we danced at Dani and Mav's wedding. I stepped on your toes, and I'm pretty sure that's what set you down the path of detesting me."

A breathy laugh escaped her throat. "I never detested you, but you were a shitty dancer. You're much better now. How?"

Clearing his throat, he appeared slightly embarrassed. "I practiced with Raquel when we were at the farm."

"Oh, that's...weird. Why?"

His dark eyes bore into hers. "I think I had a desire to dance with you again one day and not fuck it up."

Her chest rose and fell as she gazed into his eyes, unable to look away. "With Dani, you mean."

He shook his head as a flash of annoyance crossed his face. "With *you*."

"You barely knew I existed."

"That's so far from true..." Inching closer, his nose grazed hers ever so slightly. "*You're* the reason I had hope, Arianna. You always were. I knew we had a fighting chance because you were on our side."

Arianna's breath grew choppy as her heartbeat raged. "I just wanted to protect my sisters—"

His lips captured hers, swallowing her words as his tongue swirled over the tender skin behind her lower lip before surging inside. Arianna melted in his arms like a damn schoolgirl, overcome with his taste and smell. A high-pitched mewl leapt from her throat as she licked his wet tongue.

Suddenly, Arianna felt a tap on her upper back as someone loudly cleared their throat. Breaking the kiss, she twirled to find Raquel, arms crossed as she tapped her foot under a long light blue dress.

"Well, well. What do we have here?"

Chapter 21

Arianna released Dominic, tamping down the anger that surged at her sister's appearance. "What the fuck, Raquel?" she hissed. "You're working for Luthor?"

"Yes," she responded tersely. "I'm finally being appreciated for my talents and intelligence instead of being overlooked."

"Mom would be extremely disappointed in your actions and selfishness—"

"The same mother who I never got to say goodbye to because you and Dani stole her last moments from me?" Raquel extended her hands at her sides in exasperation. "Tell me again who's selfish, because that's the most selfish thing you could do to someone."

"Grow up," Arianna spat, fury in her tone. "Neither of us knew she would pass before you got to say goodbye one last time. Do you think Dani or I wanted that?"

Raquel shrugged, her shoulder-length brown hair barely touching her shoulders. "I believe you two always considered yourselves more important. Especially Dani. I'm finally out of her shadow, and I've never been happier."

Arianna studied the dark circles under her sister's green eyes and noted the hollows in her cheeks. She'd lost weight in the weeks they'd been apart, and Arianna didn't believe her bravado. "It's okay to admit you've made a mistake, Raquel. To come back with us and help Dani create a cure."

Scoffing, Raquel looked out over the now-darkened city. A muscle ticked in her jaw as she squeezed her elbows, hugging herself against the chill.

Even through all the betrayal and anger, Arianna longed to comfort her baby sister. "Raquel..." She tentatively touched her upper arm.

"Don't touch me," Raquel gritted, drawing back. "I'm not your responsibility anymore. I'm making my own life here and want to do it on my own."

"Even with the rebellion that's forming?" Dominic asked, stepping forward. "The evidence is all over the city if you choose to look. And no city can continue this level of homelessness and addiction. It won't be safe for long, Raquel."

"Then I'll die on my own terms," she said, thrusting up her chin. "I'm in the final stages of creating a diluted antidote that works wonders on addicts. It can be taken orally instead of injected and will allow people to use EverLife without withdrawal side effects."

"But they'll still be prisoners to their addiction," Arianna said, shaking her head. "That's no way to live. People need to be free of EverLife once and for all."

"Because you know what's right for everyone." Raquel rolled her eyes. "Arianna, so fucking tactical, and Dani, so fucking smart. Screw you. If people want to make the choice to take something, it's their life."

"There's no choice in addiction," Arianna said, her fist balling at her side in frustration. "You're robbing them of free will."

Straightening her shoulders, Raquel spoke without any emotion in her voice, so far from the person Arianna thought she knew. "You've lost your power to boss everyone around, Ari. If I want to work for Luthor, I will. If people want to take EverLife, they can. It's time you moved on and realized I'm done being your doormat."

Glancing toward the terrace entrance, Raquel narrowed her eyes. "You two were smart to come here instead of Dani. Luthor knows her face but not yours. Not really." Returning her gaze to Arianna's, she spoke softly. "But if I tell him my sister infiltrated the city, he's going to make you a target. Don't make me do that, Ari." Her features softened for a moment before hardening once more. "Leave and don't come back. I'm happy here."

She twirled to walk away, and Arianna caught her wrist. "Don't do this, Raquel—"

"It was done the moment you two stole her last moments from me," she said, yanking her wrist away. "Feel free to finish your dance. I guess you don't care that he's in love with Dani. I thought you had more pride than that. If you're pitiful enough to accept Dani's sloppy seconds, that's fine, but I refuse to be inferior to her anymore."

Arianna balked as if she'd been struck.

"Goodbye, Arianna. If we're lucky, this will be the last time we see each other." Raquel strode away, spine tall and majestic as a princess as Arianna gaped.

"Fucking bitch," she muttered, rubbing her forehead. "How did I never see this side of her? I'm debating running after her and punching her in her smart mouth."

"That would definitely call attention to us," Dominic said, eyes narrowed as he watched Raquel walk back inside the ballroom. "And that's the last thing we need."

Arianna sighed. "I'm going to have to forcibly remove her from this hellhole. We need to blow up Dr. Ziegler's lab so Tristan will help us. Let's do it tomorrow night so we can go on with our damn lives."

Dominic's eyes were hooded as he studied her. "Okay. Let's hang in the shadows and make contact with Matt. Maybe he discovered Tristan's address."

Her jaw was set in a firm line as she nodded.

"Don't let her get in your head," he said, sliding his palm over her lower back.

"She's not," she said, moving away from his touch. "I've always known how you feel about Dani—"

"Ari—"

"It's not a big deal," she said, cutting him off. "We need to talk to Matt and maybe Tristan if he shows up. There's nothing else to focus on but that."

Dominic's nostrils flared, and a surge of determination flashed in his dark eyes. His expression left no question that he didn't consider the conversation closed.

"We can talk about other shit when we get back to the motel. For now, I need to work this mission." She rubbed the muscles that were suddenly tense at the back of her neck. "Let's find Matt."

He tipped his head and replaced his hand at the small of her back as they headed toward the ballroom entrance. Arianna could almost feel his anger traveling through his arm into her spine. Raquel's words echoed in her head, and Arianna reminded herself that she wasn't in this for roses and love letters. She was fucking Dom to scratch an itch.

As they walked through the double doors, she hoped telling herself that would ease the ache that burned in her gut, knowing the man she loved had never wanted her first.

Annoyed at the emotion, she shut it off, determined to focus on the mission and protect her heart.

Chapter 22

Dominic stood in the darkened corner of the ballroom, aware of the change in Arianna's demeanor at Raquel's words. They'd been lodged to hurt Arianna, and Raquel knew where to hit where it hurt the most: Arianna's pride.

Dominic had rarely met someone as proud, and he cursed Raquel for pushing them back several steps. He'd made progress over the past few days, and Arianna was finally opening up to him in all the ways he craved.

Judging by the stiff set of her shoulders, they were back to square one. Just fucking great.

Imagining several inventive ways to strangle Raquel, he sipped his Scotch, reveling in the smooth taste. It had been a while since he'd had good Scotch, and since the night had gone to shit, at least he could enjoy *something*.

"There's Matt," Arianna said, her voice low as she rose to her toes. "I'm going to sidle up to him at the bar."

She was off before Dominic could respond, and he clenched his glass, frustrated she was back to making decisions without consulting him. Striding after her, he slipped into the open spot beside her as she spoke to Matt.

"What's Tristan's address?" she asked, her tone all business as Matt bristled.

"I don't know. I tried, Arianna. I made small talk with Grace at lunch and asked her where she lived before Ever-Life, but she's not really a talker. She mentioned living in the Kalorama neighborhood in the past, but that's all I got."

"No problem," Arianna said flippantly. "I've always wanted to shoot off your kneecaps. Maybe I'll put a bullet in each of your balls too. Seems fitting—"

"Okay, no one is shooting anyone," Dominic said, butting into the conversation. "And it looks like we can speak to Tristan ourselves." He gestured with his head toward the entrance as Tristan appeared. A slight frown marred his face above a pristine tuxedo as he scanned the room.

"Oh, goodie. Matt's balls are safe. For now," she finished, her tone ominous as she set off toward the entrance.

"Wait," Dominic said, leaving Matt behind as he cradled her elbow. "Let's draw him outside. I think the terrace is more inconspicuous."

"Fine." Her gaze lasered toward Tristan, and he must've felt the heat because he latched onto her, recognition in his eyes. She jerked her head toward the terrace, and Tristan gave a slight nod. Armed with his confirmation, she pivoted and walked toward the double doors that led outside.

The balcony was starting to crowd, so they headed toward the far corner, away from gossiping socialites and men in tuxedos smoking cigars. Eventually, Tristan made his way toward them, his voice hushed as he glowered. "What the fuck are you two doing here?"

"I came here for Raquel," Arianna said.

Tristan cocked a brow. "And how did that work out for you?"

"Terribly, as you seem to have already guessed. I need your address so I can forcibly remove her from the city. Now."

"We had a deal, Arianna. You blow up Dr. Ziegler's lab and then I'll tell you where she is." Rubbing his chin, he squinted one eye. "And yet, the lab is still functional and you're no closer to helping your sister. How annoying."

Arianna's fingers snaked around his neck, quick as lightning, causing him to gasp. Dominic saw him reach for the gun holstered at his belt and stepped between them.

"Enough!" Grabbing Arianna's wrist, he withdrew her hand from Tristan's throat. "You two are going to blow our cover."

Tristan stuck his finger between his collar and his rapidly bruising neck, attempting to loosen it. "I'm allowed to carry a gun since I'm one of Luthor's employees," he said to Arianna, nostrils flaring. "Don't make me use it."

"Asshole—" she hissed.

Dominic sliced his hand through the air, silently commanding Arianna to stop antagonizing him. "We're going to destroy Ziegler's lab tomorrow night. Where can we meet you the following morning to retrieve Raquel so we can get the hell out of the city?"

Tristan's eyes darted between them as he contemplated. "The corner of Connecticut and T Street. I'll be there at two a.m. and my house isn't too far away. Raquel will be sleeping and I doubt she'll go willingly."

"You let me worry about that," Arianna said.

"Fine." His shoulders lost some of their stiffness as he exhaled a deep breath. "I'm happy you're taking her out of here. Luthor just had a meeting with his security team, and he's going to start cleansing the city soon."

Arianna's eyebrows drew together. "Cleansing?"

"He plans to round up the homeless and relocate them outside the city walls. Everyone left will be required to be microchipped if they want EverLife or the watered-down antidote."

"He wants to track everyone?" Dominic asked, eyebrows drawing together.

"Yes. Tracking allows him to force compliance and implement a curfew. He wants all vestiges of the graffiti and rumors of a rebellion gone."

"But what if the rebellion is coming from inside his circle?" Arianna asked.

"The cronies who surround him are addicted to EverLife too. He assumes their continued compliance as long as he has the antidote. He controls the army and is the only one with access."

"His ego might be his downfall," Dominic said.

"I'm counting on it." Tristan's eyes glowed with resolve.

"We'll meet you at Connecticut and T at two a.m. sharp after we destroy the lab tomorrow night. Don't make us regret helping you," Arianna said.

"I think we're helping each other. Now, if I were you, I'd make myself scarce. Luthor will be here any minute, and there's nothing more for you to gain by staying. Rest up so you're fresh tomorrow night."

"I'm getting pretty fucking tired of you trying to give me orders," Arianna said, jabbing a finger in his face.

"Are George Luddington and James Stalworth on tonight's list?" Dominic asked, sliding his fingers over Arianna's forearm and slowly lowering it away from Tristan's face.

"I assume so. Why?"

"We're going to surveil them for a bit before leaving. We got a tip they might be unhappy with Luthor's claim to power."

"I could've told you that," Tristan said with a shrug. "The two fat bastards hate Luthor. But they're also rich and want to continue living their lavish lifestyle, complete with the EverLife injections that make them appear younger. I doubt they have the fortitude or wiliness to plan a rebellion."

"Then who?" Arianna asked. "Who has the skill and motive to coordinate something as complex as overthrowing Luthor?"

"That, my dear Arianna, is what I'm trying to find out."

Arianna glanced at Dominic. "Did he just call me *dear*?"

"That's our cue to end this conversation before I lose the ability to keep her from crushing your skull," Dominic said, tugging Arianna away. "Keep an eye on Luddington and Stalworth just in case there's something you might have missed. You can communicate with Arthur over the radio if you discover something."

Tristan nodded as they backed away. "Don't fail at the lab."

"Fuck you," Arianna murmured before Dominic led her away.

"Killing him won't do us any good," he said, leading them to the corner of the bar so they could observe their targets enter the party.

Dominic knew he needed to acknowledge the shift that had occurred in Arianna's demeanor after arguing with Raquel, but it would have to wait. Mission first. Then he would take her back to the motel and absolve her of the notion that she was anyone's second choice.

Tristan leaned on the bar, sipping whiskey as he surveyed the room. Raquel stood on the far side of the dance floor, chatting with two other scientists Luthor employed at the EverLife lab. Arianna and Dominic had slipped out several minutes ago, but Tristan had observed the chilled glances that passed between the sisters on their way out.

Absently staring at Raquel, he admitted it was time for her to go. If she stayed in the city after creating the antidote that she was nearly finished with, Luthor would have no need for her. He'd most likely force her out of the city with the homeless and addicted, so being removed by Arianna was the better choice.

Slightly *better*, he thought as his lips curved at Arianna's toughness. The woman was an immobile force. He hoped Dominic was channeling all that energy into something useful. If anyone needed to get laid, it was Arianna. The woman could afford to take down the intensity level several notches, and he had the sneaking suspicion Dominic might be the one man who was a match for her.

Luthor breezed through the doorway, his smooth face appearing slightly surreal since it should've long been wrinkled. Tristan noted the slight puff of his cheek bones. Swollen tissue was a side effect of EverLife, the drug that manipulated genes to keep everyone who ingested it looking young and virile.

Until it killed them by making them crave more, Tristan thought, frowning as he sipped his drink.

Jessica flanked Luthor's right side, and another woman whose name Tristan couldn't remember pressed against his left. Corinne? Kaylin? Hell if he knew. Luthor had a stable of women who traded sexual favors for EverLife and the antidote, and Tristan had stopped keeping count long ago.

Clenching his teeth, he watched Jessica rear her head back and laugh as Luthor whispered in her ear. Tristan would never be able to forgive himself for allowing his sister to be ensnared in Luthor's clutches. If he could save Raquel, perhaps it would ease some of his regret, if only slightly.

Everyone in the room rushed to meet Luthor, and he walked slowly across the dance floor, greeting his adoring fans. His security team was close behind, led by Zayne Danvers, who was excellent at ensuring Luthor lived. Tristan considered Zayne a thorn in his side since he was an obstacle in the way of murdering the bastard. But he couldn't argue that Zayne was extremely effective. The throng surrounded Luthor as he made his way to the bar, and Tristan's gaze returned to the ballroom doors.

Unable to control his quick inhale, he drank in the extra jolt of oxygen as Grace entered the room. She wore a fur coat, although he knew it was faux due to her intense love of animals. Not only dogs and cats, but when they'd been married, she'd had a ferret, a hamster and a parrot, along with the one-eyed cat she called Wink.

Tristan's pulse thrummed as he observed her smile, white teeth flashing at the attendant as she handed over her coat. Then she placed her hand over the jewels around her throat as if to protect them. The diamonds had been worth millions when the world had cared about things like elegant jewelry.

Unfortunately, his ex-wife still cared for those things. Which was why she'd married the richest man in the world. Tristan had never stood a chance.

Grace glided to the bar, seemingly unconcerned her husband was being groped by several adoring women at the other end. After ordering her customary glass of Riesling, she left the ballroom behind for the fresh air of the terrace.

Helpless to stop himself, Tristan followed her as if tethered to her by an unseen force. Scanning the dimness, he spotted her in the corner where he'd confronted Arianna and Dominic earlier. Her blond hair flitted in the breeze, long and flowing, and the curve of her hips in the white sheer gown reminded him of all the times he'd held her there...gripping her tight as he tried to control the raging lust that overwhelmed him when he made love to her.

Sometimes, he'd held her pale skin so hard that slight bruises would appear, and he would make sure to hold back the next time so he didn't scare her away. So his love for her didn't smother them both.

Sadly, no matter how much he'd tried, she'd slipped through his fingers anyway.

"The autumn nights are warm now," he said, noticing she didn't tense as he slid into place beside her. As if she knew he would eventually find his way to her.

Her fingers fiddled with the stem of the glass as she gazed over the twinkling lights of the city. "Climate change was too far gone before the world collapsed," she said, the slight gravel that always laced her voice still sexy to him after all these years. "I think fall nights will be warm for decades to come."

"Luthor's still got decades. Hell, maybe even a century or two if he keeps perfecting EverLife. So maybe he'll find a solution for climate change in the time he has left."

A huff escaped her lips. "Luthor doesn't care about those things. He just wants power."

Unable to stop himself, he traced a finger up her forearm, elated at her soft gasp. "Then you'll be the most powerful woman in the world."

Drawing her arm away, she turned and leaned her hip on the cool stone ledge. "Perhaps."

Those pink lips touched the rim of the glass, sipping as her eyes remained locked with his. "You're still protecting Raquel. I find myself wondering why."

He cocked a brow. "Maybe I have an altruistic streak."

Her features contorted acerbically. "More like a savior complex. She reminds you of Jessica."

Inhaling deeply, he nodded. "Maybe Raquel is my second chance to save someone from him."

Grace splayed her palm over her abdomen as the intensity between them simmered. Glancing down, she sharply removed her hand, as if she didn't realize she'd made the gesture.

"Our Raquel would've been born in late September," he said, glancing toward the stars since staring into her blue eyes had become unbearable. "She would've been ten this year."

Thin fingers gripped the rocky ledge, the knuckles turning white with force. "Yes. Ten years old in a world that's evil and lost. It's the only way I'm able to accept what happened, knowing she was saved from living in this world."

Tristan closed his eyes, the pain of the memories unbearable as they rushed in. Grace had been five months pregnant with their daughter—who they'd serendipitously decided to name Raquel—when the baby had suddenly been stillborn. He'd been out of the country for his last deployment, and when he returned, Grace had served him with divorce papers, stating the pain of continuing the marriage after all they'd lost was too excruciating.

"You gave up on us so easily," he said, shaking his head. "And you buried her without me. I've never forgiven you for that."

"I know." The words washed over him, filled with the grief she mostly kept hidden behind her elegant mask. "I've never forgiven myself. But Father also died, and you weren't here, and I saw the writing on the wall. I had to secure my future without him."

"I was your future," Tristan said, nostrils flaring as he clenched his jaw. "I would've taken care of you."

Leaning her elbows on the ledge, her expression grew wistful. "I was always a thing to you. A shiny object you could protect and hold in a gilded cage—"

"That's exactly how Luthor sees you, not me."

A humorless laugh escaped her throat. "You both see me that way. The difference is that Luthor is honest about it." Those gorgeous eyes latched onto his, causing his heartbeat to jolt. "I just transferred from one cage to another, but I entered the one with Luthor with eyes wide open."

Scoffing, he threw back the rest of his drink. "Well, sorry it was so shitty being married to me. Sorry I fucking loved you more than anyone on this godforsaken planet. At least you escaped the torture of being tied to me."

Her finger traced a slow, sad pattern on the ledge. "We did love each other for a time there, didn't we?"

I still love you. So goddamn much it hurts.

"Yes," he whispered, setting the glass on the stone so he didn't hurl it toward the city in anger. "For a while, it wasn't fucked up. And then, it was the three of us. Until it wasn't."

Her chin quivered as she blinked rapidly. Was she remembering the times he held her, his broad palm rubbing her belly as they tried to choose a name before he'd been deployed for that last fateful mission? The one where nothing had been the same upon his return? It was hard to tell, her face still unreadable as she stared into the blackened night.

"She would've looked just like you," he said softly. "I know it. The last thing I wanted was for her to look like an ugly wretch like me."

Breathing a laugh, she straightened, moving closer as his heart threatened to beat out of his chest. Gently cupping his jaw, she ran her thumb over the stubble. "My dear ex-husband, you are a lot of things, but ugly isn't one of them." Her cheeks flushed in the moonlight as she tenderly caressed his jaw.

He ached to reach for her...to beg her to come back to him...to ask how in the hell she could've let Luthor touch her in all the ways and places that belonged to *him*.

She dragged in a long, even breath before releasing him. "It's obvious you hate Luthor, and Jessica has no desire to be saved. I hear Arthur Reyes has one of the more functional black-market compounds, and most people know he's harboring Danica Lawson. Perhaps you should align with him. I can arrange transport for you to his compound."

"I won't leave Jessica," he said, shaking his head.

"What if I help her leave the city too?"

"The antidotes on the black-market compound are filled with shit. She needs the one here."

Grace arched a golden eyebrow. "Not if Danica is somehow working on a new antidote."

Tristan's eyes narrowed. "Where did you hear that?"

Leaning forward, she whispered, "You hear a lot when you're married to the most powerful man in the world, Tristan."

Annoyed at yet another reminder of her tether to Luthor, he grimaced. "Danica's chances of creating any sort of cure or antidote on a black-market compound are slim to none, and we both know it."

"She did it once, so her chances are better than anyone else left on the planet."

"Optimism like that will get you killed in our world, Grace. I left it behind years ago."

Backing away, she smiled. "It's not optimism, Tristan. It's *faith*, and you're terrible at it. You never had it in me, and you should have more for what lies ahead. Otherwise, what's the point of continually aligning yourself with a man you hate? Your gloom and doom mentality isn't serving you."

"It's done pretty well for me up to this point. And it's easy for a woman who wants for nothing to preach to me about faith."

Disappointment clouded her features. "I wasn't preaching, I was imploring. You're stuck so far down in the tunnel you've dug, you can't even see the light anymore."

Confusion caused him to flinch. "What the hell does that mean?"

"Mrs. Cromwell?" a voice called as a security guard dressed in a black suit approached them. "Mr. Cromwell is requesting you to be at his side as he cuts the cake."

"Of course." Facing Tristan, she smiled as her eyes roved over his face, almost as if she were memorizing his features. "Think about what I said and have some faith, Tristan. Good night."

Tristan watched her go, powerless to stop her as he'd always been. Exhausted by the cryptic conversation, he decided he'd have one more drink and then walk Raquel home so she was safe. Then, once he was alone in the confines of his bedroom, he'd try and decipher why a woman he would pledge his life to believed he had no faith.

Chapter 23

The walk back to the motel was quiet as Arianna stewed at Raquel's vitriol. The fact that her baby sister, who'd always been kind and loving, had devolved into the person on the terrace tonight was extremely disheartening. Perhaps the world truly was too far gone and all vestiges of goodness were slowly eroding.

And Raquel's words about Dominic? They were a good reminder for Arianna to protect her heart. No matter how much she loved him, she'd never come close to forever with any man. Experience had shown her it was impossible, and the fear that Dominic would ultimately realize that welled in her chest.

She could fuck him and even share some intimacies, but giving herself completely was off the table. She needed to focus, and being shattered by Dominic would derail her goals.

They climbed up the stairs to their room, Dominic simmering behind her, and she reminded herself to stay calm. Impassive. Unemotional. Sure, she would still have sex with him tonight—after all, sex with Dominic was incredible, and she wasn't ready to deny herself some small sliver of pleasure in their fucked-up world.

But that's as far as it would go. Meaningless sex to release some tension. Lord knew she could use it.

They entered the dim room, and Arianna walked to the small table where their guns rested. Leaning on it, she removed her shoes and rubbed her foot to soothe the sting. For someone who often wore combat boots or sneakers, flat dress shoes were an unwelcome change.

"Let's get up at sunrise to jog," she said, attempting to make normal conversation and ignore the ticking of Dominic's jaw as he tugged off his shoes, jacket and bow tie before removing his shirt and tossing it on the couch. "And if you want to fuck, that's fine, but let's make it quick because I'm beat—"

Her words were cut off as Dominic lifted her over his shoulder, knocking her breath from her lungs as he carried her to the bedroom. Shock pervaded her system as she realized how easily he maneuvered her body atop his shoulder. She was not a small woman by any means, and no man had ever had the strength—or the nerve—to manhandle her.

When they reached the bedroom, he tossed her on the bed, her back hitting the comforter as she gaped up at him. "For fuck's sake, Dom. I can walk—"

"Shut up," he demanded, straddling her and pressing his palms on both sides of her head. Arianna's heart pounded with equal parts desire and anger.

"You're the first man who's ever told me to shut up, and I swear, each time you do it, I debate letting you live."

His palm snaked around her throat, surrounding her gasp as he held her immobile. Not too hard, but firm enough that she knew who was in control. Fuck. How had she let him have control when she'd spent the entire walk home deciding to play it cool? Annoyed at how easily he played her...how much he understood her...she tried like hell to keep her muscles rigid. Tough, since every instinct in her body wanted to relax under his soft domination.

Never had she wanted to give herself to someone and let them have complete control.

Never before *him.*

"You want to turn this into something it isn't," he said, his voice low with the hum of anger and frustration. "Some quick fucks to burn off energy."

"That's all it is—"

"No." His hand tightened on her neck, causing her eyes to roll back in her head with pleasure. Damn it. She fucking loved having his thick fingers around her neck. The war between her emotions and her self-preservation raged inside her rapidly heating frame as she lay beneath him.

"Look at me, Arianna."

She lifted her lids, stifling the urge to simultaneously kick him in the balls and beg him to love her back. God, her feelings for this man defied logic and upended every sense of her carefully cultivated self-control.

"Stop letting Raquel's words inside that hard head." He tapped her forehead with his free hand. "You have to let go of this notion that my feelings for you are in any way equivalent to what I felt for Dani. I refuse to keep having this same argument...or discussion...or whatever it is that makes you doubt what's happening here."

"Nothing's happening," she rasped. "We both deserve a release."

"A release?" he asked incredulously. "What you don't understand, Ari, is that I don't just need to fuck you. I need to *worship* you."

He dropped to his knees beside the bed, gripping her behind the knees and dragging her forward. When her ass hit the edge, he roughly tore the dress from her body. Cool air hit her breasts as he yanked her underwear down her legs and tossed it aside.

"Maybe if I make you scream, you'll admit what's between us." Draping her legs over his shoulders, he pressed his palms to her inner thighs. Pushing them open, his dark eyes blazed as he stared at her. "Watch me worship you, Arianna. My gorgeous, fearless warrior."

Arianna whimpered as he slowly lowered his lips to her abdomen, kissing a trail to her navel and dipping his tongue inside.

"Dom..."

"All you have to do is stay right there and enjoy this." His mouth trailed over the skin between her navel and the top of her mound, causing the skin to quiver beneath. "I'm not Matt or any of the other men you've done this with. I'm someone who gets you, Arianna. Someone who can handle you. And you're about to get fucking handled, sweetheart."

His fingers touched her slick folds before gently pulling them apart. Eyes locked with hers, he blew on her damp flesh, the sight more erotic than any Arianna had ever seen. His full lips glistened as he licked them, as if he was preparing to savor the finest dish.

"You're mine, Arianna. This pussy is *mine*. And I'm going to claim it in the way you deserve."

Her hands flew to his head, gripping since she ached to touch him. His hair was short, so there was barely anything to cling on to, but she squeezed anyway, her fingers digging into his flesh.

"Good girl. Hold on tight."

Why did her body inflame every time he called her that? Why did she crave it with him unlike any other man she'd ever known?

"Because you're mine," he said, nuzzling her slit as he read her thoughts. Closing his eyes, he inhaled a deep breath. "Fuck, I love your scent, Ari." Then all talking ceased as he buried his face in her quivering core.

His talented tongue swiped a path from her opening to her clit, causing Arianna's legs to tremble around his head as she groaned. Holding her open, he flicked the swollen bud, over and over, before drawing it between his lips. He sucked her in a deep, fluid motion, stimulating the frayed nerve endings.

"Oh god!"

His murmured "*mmm*" vibrated against her as she rocked into his mouth. Unable to control her hips, she undulated toward him, seeking the pleasure he unselfishly offered.

As his tongue continued the pleasurable ministrations, he pressed a finger to her opening, circling the damp ring before nudging inside. Arianna's head fell back on the bed, her body racked with pleasure as she welcomed his invasion.

He slid deep inside her, searching for the bundle of nerves that sat deep within. When she gasped, he released a groan and inserted another finger...then one more. He stretched her, sliding in and out as his mouth worked her clit, and Arianna moaned his name.

"No more walls," he said, lapping at her core as he fucked her in smooth strokes with his fingers. "I want all of you, Ari."

Her muscles went lax at his words, her defenses unable to remain against the blissful onslaught from his mouth and fingers. She sensed his body's change at her acquiescence. The way his shoulders sagged beneath her legs, as if silently accepting she'd finally let go.

The flicks of his tongue drove her to the point of madness as the pads of his fingers found the spot deep within that all others had failed to discover. Craving the pleasure, she let him have it all, opening her legs in wide invitation as he devoured her.

Moans laced her scattered, shallow breaths as she reached for the pinnacle. Every cell of her skin burned with pleasure, aching for release. Spearing her short nails into Dominic's head, she held on for dear life as tiny whimpers she'd never emitted for any other man leapt from her throat.

Suddenly, her back arched and her eyes glazed over before her eyelids began to flutter. Wave upon glorious wave of pleasure crashed through her frame as Dominic led her to the most magnificent orgasm she'd ever experienced.

Her body bucked and bowed, the slick honey between her legs flowing under his warm mouth, and she emitted a passionate wail, wishing the bliss would never end.

Finally, after the universe exploded and somehow reassembled itself, her muscles turned to jelly upon the bed. Lax and sated, she tried to open her eyes but couldn't find the strength.

Dominic's sigh heated the skin between her legs as they quaked around his head. All sense of control was shattered, and damn, she fucking loved it.

He slowly stood and removed the rest of his clothes before lifting her and positioning her properly on the bed. Turning off the lamp they'd left illuminated on the bedside table, he crawled in behind her. Drawing her close, he spooned her and buried his face in the soft skin behind her neck.

Arianna wiggled the globes of her ass into his hard cock, offering herself to him as she lay spent and frazzled.

"I just want to hold you," he murmured, sliding his arm between her breasts and cupping her throat with that broad hand. Fuck. His hand around her throat was quickly becoming her favorite addiction.

"I don't cuddle," she murmured, her lips twitching in anticipation of his denial of her words.

"You do with me." His hand gently squeezed her neck as tiny bumps of resulting pleasure prickled her skin.

"Holy shit, Dom. You destroyed me."

Full lips kissed her neck as he draped a thick thigh over hers. "I worshiped you in the way you need, Ari. In the way I *crave*. You're not my second choice. You're my first obsession. Now let me sleep, woman. You tired me out."

Arianna swallowed thickly, counting his slowing heartbeats as they thumped across her back. With each breath, she felt the locks and bolts that protected her heart shatter as they slowly disintegrated and disappeared.

Dominic's skillful tongue and reverent words were massively effective at destroying the carefully built walls she'd erected. Soon, there would be nothing left to deny him from consuming her and annihilating her if he ever decided she wasn't enough...if he ever decided to leave her as so many others had. Her birth parents. Her adoptive parents. Every man she'd ever thought she'd loved. Even her baby sister... They all left eventually, didn't they? Was it foolish to think this time could be different?

She waited for the metallic taste of fear to coat her tongue. When it didn't appear, she took a moment to acknowledge the emotion that welled within, realizing it felt like...relief. Somehow, for once, fear and love weren't inexorably interwoven together in the deepest corners of her heart. She just felt...*free*.

And that, she realized, was something she'd need time to grapple with. It was new and daunting, and her exhausted body needed rest to fully accept it. Allowing herself to relax, she shimmied into Dominic's warm frame as he held her in the dark.

Chapter 24

Dani assembled the syringe, gauze, vial and other components on the sterile blue sheet atop the rolling metal cart. Noticing the slight shake in her gloved hands, she took a deep breath to calm herself.

"You've got this, slugger," Maverick said, cupping her shoulder with a supportive squeeze. "And if this round doesn't work, we'll make more until we find a cure."

Dani smiled up at him, grateful for his unending encouragement. "You know, for someone who destroyed the world, I have an extremely supportive husband. I still wonder sometimes why you didn't throw in the towel when I initiated the downfall of society."

"Who else is going to accept a guy named after a cheesy eighties movie?" he teased, kissing her forehead. "I'll be right here, babe."

Scrunching her nose, she lifted the syringe and stuck it in the vial, withdrawing the milky fluid as she chided him. "And then you call me 'babe' and I debate leaving you forever."

He covered his heart as his lips formed a broad smile. "You wound me, Dr. Lawson-Ward." Backing away, he whispered "Good luck" before leaning against the wall and crossing his arms.

Inhaling a fortifying breath, Dani approached the woman lying on the infirmary bed. Shallow breaths flowed through her chapped lips as she stared at the ceiling with unseeing eyes. Dani noticed the large pupils, surrounded by red-dened vessels, and the dark bags formed on the skin underneath.

"Hi, Sarah. My name is Danica and I'm here to help you," she said encouragingly, gently surrounding the woman's arm and placing it flat so the veins of her inner arm were exposed. Dragging the medical cart closer, she set the syringe on top and wet a piece of gauze with alcohol. After cleaning Sarah's skin, she wrapped a rubber tourniquet around her upper arm.

Dani tapped Sarah's arm, causing the veins to stand to attention. Identifying the most prominent one, she lifted the syringe and placed the tip of the needle on Sarah's arm.

"This will pinch a bit, but otherwise, it shouldn't hurt." Narrowing her eyes, she focused as she injected the milky serum into Sarah's arm.

Her patient's chest lifted as she inhaled a deep breath, and Dani took it as a good sign she was eliciting any reaction at all. Once the syringe was empty, she set it on the tray and removed the tourniquet. Massaging Sarah's arm, she waited, observing her reaction.

The woman's long brown eyelashes began to move as she blinked once...twice...and then more rapidly. The pulse at her neck fluttered visibly as Dani's eyes widened.

"Sarah? My name is Danica, and I just injected your arm with some medicine. You're okay." She held her forearm in a firm, comforting grasp as Sarah's eyes met hers. They were laced with confusion and fear.

"You've been addicted to EverLife and then you took an antidote that had some nasty stuff in it. Your body was under attack, but I just injected you with something that should help. How do you feel?"

Sarah's jaw worked as she tried to speak. "Where's Jenny? And Christopher?"

Smiling, Dani rubbed her thumb in gentle strokes over her skin. "Your kids are safe. They've been staying at the shelter Arthur set up for kids of addicted parents."

"Arthur Reyes? I remember him building walls around the site... Everyone was dying and we needed more antidote..."

"He's been trying to keep you all alive, but it's been tough. That's why I'm trying to help."

Leaning back on the bed, she exhaled a deep breath. "I feel...better. I'm not..."—she smacked her lips—"...craving EverLife." Turning her head on the pillow, she looked at Dani. "How?"

Glancing at Maverick, Dani felt elation surge at her words. "Go get the nurse so she can monitor Sarah's vitals," she said, her tone firm. "And then gather the team so we can pick more plants and replicate the serum. We need fifty vials immediately."

Maverick nodded and quickly left the room.

"Danica?"

"It's okay," she said, rubbing Sarah's arm. "It's possible the serum has quelled the addiction. If you continue to improve, I'll test the antidote on other patients in the clinic."

Sarah licked her parched lips. "And if it works on them too?"

Dani's mouth curved into a huge smile. "Then we're on our way to eliminating this fucking curse of a drug from the planet."

Her eyes closed in relief. "Thank God."

Dani backed away as Chris and Jenny ran into the room, followed by Maverick and one of the nurses, Rikina, who'd helped keep the clinic afloat in their squalid dystopian circumstances. Sliding her arm around Maverick's waist, Dani watched the reunion, allowing hope to surge. She wasn't sure if there were any gods left to thank, but damn it, she'd do her best to ensure everyone in the clinic—and the world—would have the ability to pray to whichever one they chose.

CHAPTER 25

After a brisk sunrise jog, Dominic and Arianna headed back to the motel to shower and plan. They spread Tristan's map of the lab over the small coffee table and discussed their prior surveillance.

"After Guard One leaves for his break, we'll shoot Guard Two with the tranquilizer dart and enter." Her finger traveled the path to the main lab on the map. "Then we'll detonate the explosives here." She tapped her finger.

"We'll need to leave through the back entrance," Dominic said, touching the map. "It's labeled exit only, but that's all we need."

Nodding, Arianna blew out a breath, ruffling the hair above her forehead. The bald side of her head was growing in, and Dominic thought it made her look exotic...and sexy.

"You're looking at me like you want to eat me," she said, and his lips curved at her teasing tone. Something had changed between them last night, and he relished the easy energy that pulsed between them.

"I think we've established that I like eating you."

She rolled her eyes as a faint smile tugged at her mouth. "So fucking cheesy. Gross."

Chuckling, he placed his palm over her thigh, unable to resist touching her. "Want to get some lunch from the deli?"

"Yes. I want to ask Deandra to watch out for Raquel if we fail."

Dominic squeezed her leg. "We won't, but I like the sentiment."

As they waited for Ron to cook the roast beef sandwiches, Arianna spoke softly to Deandra as she stood behind the counter.

"I'm not thrilled at keeping an eye out for the person creating Luthor's super drug, but I have a soft spot for you two." She patted Arianna's cheek. "I'll watch out for her. But don't die, all right? I need to know there are people like you in the world, Arianna."

"I'll do my best," Arianna said, taking the bag that Ron handed her. "And thank you." Reaching into her pack, she removed three gold bars.

"Oh, this is too much," Deandra said, pushing them away.

"You deserve more, but it's all I can give now." Arianna shoved them into her hands. "One day, I hope to return your kindness in every way I can."

Deandra's brown eyes grew teary as she hugged the bars to her chest. "Be safe. And when you return to take down Luthor, I'll be here ready to help you."

Arianna hugged her as Dominic tipped his head to both her and Ron before giving a salute. Ron saluted back, a relic of his time in the US Army when it had still existed.

After lunch, Dominic tugged Arianna close as they sat on the couch, urging her to curl into his side.

"I'm not used to this," she said, snuggling into his chest. "Don't you just want to have sex?"

He smoothed his palm over her hair, loving the texture of her braid beneath his skin. "Tell me what you want after we're done fighting."

Her fingers toyed with the prickly hairs that sprang from underneath his collar. "I want Dani to regain all her memories and live happily ever after with Mav."

"What else?"

"I want Raquel to come back to us and finally grow into the person I know she can be."

He ran his cheek over her hair. "Keep going."

"I want a daughter that has my mama's eyes. I don't remember much about her, but for some reason, I remember her eyes. They had these golden flecks in them that shone in the sunlight and crinkled around them when she smiled."

Arianna had the same eyes, filled with the same flecks between the swirls of green and brown. Dominic thought them stunning and could imagine a daughter with them.

"I want a boy, so we'll have to have two."

"*Pfft*," she exclaimed, squeezing him even as she discounted his words. "I told you, I'm using a turkey baster. It won't require the effort of dealing with someone else."

Sliding his fingers under her chin, he forced her to meet his gaze. "I'm under the impression that you enjoy our *efforts* together." He arched a confident brow.

"God, I hate that smug smile." Touching two fingers to the top of his scar, she tenderly traced them down the length of the gash. Over his nose...down to the corner of his lips, following the trail of the machete that had initially made the mark.

Dominic nipped her finger. "I think you love it. I think you love *me*."

Her breath stuttered as her eyes darted back and forth between his. "That's another reason I want a baby," she said softly, ignoring his bold statement. "I think I can love her...or him"—her lips quirked—"and not be afraid."

"You've lost a lot," he said, cupping her jaw. "We both have. It makes us fiercely protective of what remains."

"Protecting Dani and Raquel is nothing compared to how I would protect my child. Once she's here, I'll make sure she's loved and cherished in every way she deserves."

"I understand," he said, tracing his thumb over her bottom lip, "because that's exactly the way I want to protect you."

Challenge flared in her eyes, and he covered her lips before she could speak. "Instead of arguing with me about not needing anyone's protection, why don't you just let me hold you and imagine the day when you finally get what you want?"

Sighing, she buried her head into the juncture of his neck and chest. Dominic felt her body relax as he softly stroked her shoulder. In a few hours, they would be thrust into yet another mission full of danger where their very existence was on the line.

But for now, he was content to hold her and imagine himself in the future she longed to create.

Chapter 26

After it grew dark, they dressed in their black tactical gear, each strapping weapons to accessible parts of their muscular frames. They had the tranquilizer guns, the handguns they'd brought with them, and the semi-automatic rifles they'd taken from the two guards at the wall.

When they were strapped and ready, Dominic's gaze traveled over Arianna, his throat bobbing as his heart skipped a beat. She stood tall, with that half-mane of hair braided over her shoulder. Weapons lined her sides and the bronze skin of her arms showed off the sinewy muscle beneath.

Shifting in her black boots, her eyebrows narrowed. "What?"

Striding toward her, he grabbed her chin and kissed her. "You're fucking gorgeous. Let's go."

She looked down her body as her eyebrows ticked up. "This *is* pretty hot, if you're into kick-ass chicks."

Dominic chuckled and walked to the door, turning to peruse the room. "We'll just leave it unlocked since we're not coming back, right? I left the key on the coffee table."

"Yep. I left one gold bar for Devon on the table too. Hope he uses it for something productive instead of a vial of EverLife." She followed him across the threshold and pulled the door closed.

The trek to the lab would take two hours, and they remained mostly silent as they walked. Dominic knew she was as focused as he was on getting in, completing the mission, and then meeting up with Tristan so they could locate Raquel and get the hell out of the city.

When they finally reached the lab, they perched atop the hill that allowed visibility to the guards below. As expected, the first guard left for his break at midnight.

Arianna turned to him from her crouched position behind a large tree and gestured with her head toward the facility.

Dominic nodded and they both sprang forward, maneuvering down the hill to take out the remaining guard.

Arianna lifted the tranquilizer gun, her grip steady as she aimed, and Dominic found himself entranced as always by her skillful handling of the weapon. Her finger settled over the trigger before pulling, and a moment later, a dart landed in the guard's neck. He grasped the entrance wound and sucked in a breath before falling to the ground.

They charged forward, Dominic lowering to yank the badge from the man's chest. He swiped it over the keypad, and green light illuminated as the pad beeped. Turning the handle, he tugged open the door, and they entered.

"Stay close," Arianna commanded, turning on her flashlight and leading the way. Dominic didn't argue since he trusted her without hesitation. Although his protective streak inwardly rebelled, he knew she was the finest soldier he would ever partner with. Hell, he'd follow her into battle in any scenario, and this one was no different.

They snaked their way through the lab, the hair raising on the back of Dominic's neck as they grew closer to where the serum was stored. Something about the raid was too...*easy*, and it sent a jolt of nervous awareness down his spine.

Arianna reached the lab door, and Dominic handed her the guard's badge. She slid it over the keypad and the deadbolt clicked. Pushing the door, they headed inside the sterile lab.

Metal tables scattered the room, some covered with cages that held mice and other test animals. Arianna approached the middle of the lab and pointed at the vials that sat beside a microscope.

"Let's place the explosives here and plant more through-out the room. We can use the detonator from the hallway and then head for the back exit."

Dominic nodded as they both removed their backpacks.

Suddenly, the sound of a vial shattering caused them both to whirl toward the entrance. A man appeared, tall and dressed in black, holding a semi-automatic rifle. Dominic reached for his gun, but the man shook his head.

"I wouldn't do that, Dominic. I'm Luthor's head of securi-ty, and we're holding Raquel in his penthouse as we speak. If one bullet flies from either of your guns, I give the order to kill her." He tapped the comm device in his ear. "So, you two either come with me or she dies."

Arianna's shoulders deflated. "It's a set up."

"Of course it's a set up," the man sneered. "Do you think Luthor would let you destroy his next great drug?" His eyes remained locked on them as he called over his shoulder, "Secure them and load them onto the convoy."

Two Sen Force soldiers rushed in, and Arianna looked at Dominic with equal parts anger and terror in those stun-ning eyes.

"Stay strong," he said as the soldiers approached. "He won't kill us or Raquel until he has information on Arthur and Dani."

Arianna nodded quickly before the soldiers drew their arms behind their backs, securing them with zip ties. Then a black bag was shoved over Dominic's head, and a painful blow lodged at his temple before everything faded to black.

Chapter 27

T ristan stood in Luthor's penthouse home, remarking on how cold and sterile it was. One would think that a home would have some warmth, but the space was as devoid of character and ambience as his penthouse office several blocks away. Expansive windows lined the room as the city lights twinkled outside.

Raquel Lawson sat on the spacious couch in the middle of the staid living room, fire in her eyes as she glared at Tristan above the gag he'd shoved in her mouth. He hadn't wanted to scare her, but he had a plan and she played an integral part in it.

And if all went well, she'd be leaving with Arianna and Dominic, which he still firmly believed was best for her.

Zayne Danvers, the head of Luthor's security team, thrust open the double doors and entered the room with four members of his security team close behind. They wheeled Dominic and Arianna to the couch, setting them on either side of Raquel before gliding the wheelchairs to the corner. Then they assumed their places along the wall by the entrance, waiting for their next orders as Luthor addressed Zayne.

"How long did it take them to realize it was a setup?" Luthor asked.

"Not long. They didn't put up a fight when they heard we had Raquel."

"Good." Walking toward his captives, Luthor lifted Raquel's chin as she squirmed and shrieked behind the gag. "Such a sassy little thing. You've done good work in the lab, Raquel, and I appreciate it. I won't kill you, but I need you to do something for me."

She shook her head as Luthor formed a sinister sneer. Releasing her, he spoke to Zayne. "Wake them up."

Zayne gave a nod to one of the guards, who strode toward the couch with two vials in his hands. He injected one in Dominic's arm and one in Arianna's, who jolted to consciousness and yelled a muffled "What the fuck?" under her black hood.

Luthor approached and removed the hoods as Arianna struggled with the binds behind her back and at her ankles.

"Relax, Arianna. It's just a mild stimulant to wake you both up. I might pump you both full of EverLife soon, but it's not time for that yet," he said ominously, cocking a dark eyebrow.

"You know, I only *wanted* to kill you before this," Arianna spat. "Now, I'm *definitely* going to kill you."

Get in line, Tristan thought as he assessed the situation. For his plan to work, he'd need the two Sen Force soldiers he'd paid handsomely standing against the far wall to do their part. They weren't members of Zayne's security force, and both had small kids they needed to feed, so they were open to bribery. But first, Tristan needed to catch Luthor and Zayne unaware. A difficult task since Luthor was wily and Zayne was an exceptional guard.

"Your sister is the one I want to inject with EverLife in real time for everyone to see," Luthor said, slowly pacing as he spoke. "It's a fitting end to the villain's story. And before you point out that I'm the villain, I'll let you know that I agree."

Arianna glared at him before glancing over at Raquel and Dominic, concern in her gaze.

"The old world made me a villain with its insistence on limiting my power," Luthor continued. "If the government had just realized I was imperative to its success, everything would've been easier."

"You're a fucking plague on the world, and I won't let you near Dani!"

"That's a shame, because having you lead me to her is my master plan." Moving closer, he pointed at Raquel. "You see, I'll kill *her* if you don't. And I don't think you'll let that happen."

"What's the plan, then?" Dominic asked. "We return to Arthur's compound and you ambush him?"

"Yes," Luthor said with a nod. "You'll show up at the compound walls, and they'll open the gates, never knowing there are hundreds of Sen Force soldiers waiting in the surrounding woods."

"Fuck that. I'd rather die," Arianna said.

"But I don't think you'd let Raquel die," he said, lifting a finger. "In fact, I'm counting on it." Lifting the gun from the holster at his waist, he pressed it to Raquel's temple. "Or am I wrong?"

"Wait!" Arianna yelled, shaking her head. "Let's negotiate. There has to be a way we can help you and both of my sisters live."

Sheathing the gun, Luthor rubbed his chin. "I relish the idea of publicly injecting Dani with EverLife and allowing her to die from the side effects, but..." His eyes narrowed as he arched an eyebrow. "Capturing Arthur Reyes is the ultimate prize. His support grows alongside talk of a rebellion. His compound walls are heavily guarded, and his hackers rival mine even though they barely have access to technology. I've yet to figure out a way in besides bombing from the air, and the people in the cities are so tired of war and death."

"I see the fear in your eyes, Cromwell," Dominic said. "The people in the cities are tired of *you*. You're afraid if you bomb Reyes's compound, the rebellion that's forming will have the final push it needs."

Luthor's nose wrinkled. "Rebellion is such a dirty word, especially since I'm not a dictator. I'm a leader. One who's fair and just to those who deserve it."

"Rich assholes, you mean?" Arianna scoffed.

"People who worked hard to create something to better the world!" Luthor jabbed his finger at the darkened windows. "Everyone out there is happy. They look and feel younger, and they have everything they need. I created that!"

"You're delusional," Arianna said. "I knew that, but it's worse that I imagined."

"Enough talking," Luthor said, slicing his hand through the air. "Tristan will accompany you to Arthur's compound to ensure your compliance. I know Arthur wants to make contact with him, so he won't suspect anything when you show up with Tristan at your side."

Arianna's nostrils flared as her gaze flew to Tristan's. "Traitor," she hissed.

"I told you I have my own goals, Arianna. Sorry they don't align with yours."

"Zayne, you'll assign a guard to Raquel and hold her in my guest room as discussed," Luthor said, grabbing Raquel's wrist and tugging her to her feet. He shoved her toward Zayne and she crashed into his body, her bound feet barely holding her up as her knuckles scraped her lower back.

Suddenly, her head snapped toward Tristan, and he stared deep into her eyes, giving a faint nod. Zayne pushed her to his side as Luthor continued talking to Arianna and Dominic about his plan to approach Arthur's compound while the soldiers hid in the nearby forest.

Raquel's fingers closed around the small box cutter Tristan had slid into the back pocket of the jeans he'd forced her to don at gunpoint when he'd awoken her in his home. Those light green eyes shot daggers at him as she'd dressed before he tied her feet and ankles and gagged her...and surreptitiously slipped the makeshift weapon into her back pocket.

Tristan knew she wouldn't be searched if she was bound, and it was the only way to get her into the penthouse while in possession of a weapon.

She blended into the background, as she often complained of doing, while Luthor droned on. Using slow, deft movements, she sawed the zip tie holding her wrists. Tristan glanced at the two Sen Force soldiers along the back wall, ensuring they were prepared to defend him if things took a turn for the worst. They stood silent, their hands crossed at their belts as Raquel broke free.

"You see, Arianna," Luthor said, approaching Raquel and waving Zayne away. Zayne moved to stand by the security guard near the door and assumed a watchful stance as Luthor cupped Raquel's shoulder. "Your younger sister doesn't hold the importance of Dr. Danica Lawson, but you know you can't leave her here to die—"

Suddenly, Raquel jabbed the box cutter forward, impaling it in Luthor's side as he wailed. His knees buckled, and he collapsed on the carpet as all hell broke loose.

Raquel rushed over to Arianna, using the box cutter to saw off her restraints before moving to Dominic. Zayne pulled his gun from his belt and aimed at Raquel.

"Should I shoot her, sir?"

Luthor held up a hand as he slowly rose to his feet, wheezing in pain. "No. I think public torture would be better. Take all three of them into custody."

Zayne stepped forward, and something clicked in Tristan's brain.

Ice circulated through his veins as the world seemed to spin in slow motion. Feeling as if he was envisioning the actions from outside his body, Tristan observed Zayne turn away from Raquel. Holding the gun with firm purpose, he lifted it high and aimed it at...Luthor.

"Actually, Luthor, I think it's time *you're* the one who's arrested."

Luthor's eyes grew wide as he sucked in a breath. "You?" he rasped. "You're the leader of the rebellion?"

Tristan remained silent, his heartbeat roaring in his ears as Zayne spoke over his shoulder. "Take Luthor into custody," he commanded his security team.

Tristan watched, stunned. He'd heard grumblings that the rebellion might be formed from people in Luthor's inner circle, but he'd never suspected Zayne.

"Think long and hard about the decision you're about to make," Luthor warned Zayne's security team. "I'm the leader of the army and the most powerful man in the world. The Sen Force soldiers stationed in every lab and warehouse in this city have orders to destroy all inventory if I die. Any of your family members addicted to EverLife will lose the precious antidote they need."

The security guards looked between each other, and Tristan's finger itched upon the trigger. It would be so easy to kill Luthor, right here, right now. But then Jessica would lose the antidote, and until Dani had created something accessible, he wouldn't chance her life.

Tristan noticed an almost imperceptible movement out of the corner of his eye and realized Raquel was pressing the box cutter into Arianna's hand. *Smart girl.* Arianna was much more dangerous with a weapon and could possibly catch Luthor unaware in the surrounding chaos.

Zayne barked more orders at his men to seize Luthor, and they remained still, the gravity of the decision looming on their faces.

Suddenly, Grace trailed through the door, her eyes heavy from sleep and her expression perplexed. "What the hell is going on in here? I heard yelling—"

Zayne seized the opportunity, snatching her against his body and planting the barrel of the gun against her temple. "No one move or I'll kill her."

Tristan aimed his gun at Zayne's head although he wasn't able to get a clean shot with Grace struggling in his arms. She squirmed and kicked, but her efforts were no match for the large man holding her hostage.

"We both know you need her alive, Luthor," Zayne said, backing out of the room. "George Luddington only supports you because of Grace. She'll come in handy as we work to sway him to the rebellion's side." Stepping across the threshold, he pulled the doors closed and something rattled on the other side.

Tristan rushed to the doors, attempting to yank them open, but they wouldn't budge. "The bastard locked them from outside. Fuck!" He slammed his palm on the door in frustration.

Arianna rushed toward Luthor, holding the box cutter high before rearing back in pain and clutching her arm. "What the—?"

One of Zayne's remaining security guards fired at Arianna, making contact with her upper arm. Raquel screamed and jolted toward her, lowering to her knees as Arianna fell to the floor. "Ari? Are you okay?"

"Shoot them!" Luthor commanded.

Raquel picked up the box cutter and rushed toward Luthor, lifting it high to strike. Sadly, she never stood a chance. Several bullets lodged in her body before she collapsed on the ground, her gray shirt rapidly turning red with blood.

Bullets flew at Tristan, and he lunged behind the large chair several feet away, taking cover as the security team surrounded Luthor before dragging him toward the door. One of the men kicked it several times and it flew open. They dragged Luthor out and away to safety.

Tristan rose and spoke to the Sen Force soldiers he'd recruited to his side. "We just need two minutes to get out of the building and into the Jeep waiting below. Go home to your families and don't tell anyone that Zayne is the leader of the rebellion."

They both nodded before exiting.

Tristan heard Arianna's soft pleading as she bent over her sister's dying body. It appeared that one bullet had only grazed Arianna's arm, but Raquel wasn't so lucky. Tentatively approaching, Tristan touched Arianna's shoulder.

"We have to go. Dominic can carry her to the Jeep."

Raquel's eyes glazed over as she stared up at Arianna. "I'm so sorry," she whispered, her skin turning pale as snow as she bled out. "I just wanted to be special for once."

"You are," Arianna said, tears streaming from her eyes as she cupped Raquel's face. "You've always been special to me and Dani. I don't know why you didn't believe it."

Raquel inhaled a long breath before her eyes slid closed. "You have to win. Tell Dani I'm sorry. And tell her bromantane is the main ingredient in Dr. Ziegler's drug."

"You tell her yourself," Arianna said, stroking her cheek. Raquel exhaled a slow, ragged breath before all signs of life left her sagging muscles. "Damn it, Raquel! You tell her yourself!" Arianna slapped her cheek, but it was no use.

"Ari," Dominic said, gently tugging her hand away. "We have to go. I'll carry her." He lifted Raquel's lifeless body and faced Tristan. "Are you coming with us?"

Tristan shook his head. "I need to find Grace. That's my first priority. After tonight, Luthor will most likely begin using the super drug on his soldiers and start attacking the compounds. Arthur's will surely be first. Tell him to contact me on the radio."

"Are you going to align with Zayne and the rebellion?" Dominic asked as he moved toward the door.

"I don't know. I need to scope out the situation and save Grace. You must know by now that she's my wife..." Swiping a hand over his face, he sighed. "My *ex*-wife. But she's not trained in any sort of combat and is completely helpless. Saving her will be my main priority. Once I accomplish that, I can focus on what happens next. Come on. We've got to get out of here."

They entered the elevator, whooshing to the lobby and the black Jeep parked outside.

"Take it while you still can," Tristan said. "Luthor will send men down here any minute. I bribed the two guards at the Francis Scott Key Bridge crossing who will let you through."

"Thank you. Your foresight is what's keeping me from beating the shit out of you for setting us up," Dominic said.

"It needed to be done" was Tristan's flippant response. "We've set something in motion now that can't be stopped. I hope you all are ready for a war. I'll be in touch...and I'm very sorry about Raquel." With a salute, he skulked off into the night.

Dominic loaded Raquel into the back seat, and Arianna climbed in to hold her. Revving the engine, Dominic drove fast as lightning toward the edge of the city, leaving DC behind.

Chapter 28

Arianna stroked her sister's hair, her head resting in her lap as they neared Arthur's compound. When they pulled up to the gate, Dominic exited the car and extended his arms, allowing the searchlights to rove over him. Once he was cleared, the heavy metal doors swung open and they drove inside.

"Please wait here," one of the guards said. "We have strict orders that Arthur has to personally approve your re-entrance to the compound."

Dominic opened the back door of the Jeep, his heart breaking at the sight of Arianna's tender ministrations on Raquel's hair.

"Ari," he softly called. "It's time for you to let her go, sweetheart. We'll ask Arthur to have the nurses at the infirmary clean and prepare her body."

Arianna's chin warbled as she nodded. "Don't let Dani see her like this, covered in blood."

"Okay."

After slowly releasing her, Arianna took the hand he offered and climbed out of the Jeep. Gazing up at him, she wiped her nose. "I was supposed to save her, Dom."

"It's not your fault, Arianna." Drawing her into a firm hug, he stroked her back as they waited for Arthur. Eventually, he appeared in one of the compound's run-down pickup trucks, his expression thoughtful as he approached.

"I assume things went badly if you two are consoling each other."

"They went really fucking badly," Arianna said, turning to face him. "Raquel is dead and Luthor knows who's leading the rebellion. He's planning on creating an army of drug-induced super soldiers, and your compound will be the first he attacks."

"Shit." Arthur rubbed his forehead. "How much time do you think we have to prepare?"

"Could be days, could be weeks," Dominic said. "But we'd be better prepared if we could track down the rebellion leader and have them fight with us."

"Agreed. Who is the leader?"

"Zayne Danvers, Luthor's head of security. He's taken Luthor's wife hostage, so Tristan is searching for them too. Perhaps you can make contact with him on the radio frequency and Arianna and I can help him search. We'll cover more ground if we combine our efforts."

"Okay." Peering into the car, Arthur frowned. "Do you all want a burial or a cremation?"

"A burial, please," Arianna said. "If you can take care of preparing her body, I'd like to plan an afternoon funeral on the hill behind the middle school. The four of us need to mourn her, even if she betrayed us."

"I'll have the body ready within a few hours." Lifting his hand high, he circled it and several men jogged over. Arthur whispered hushed directions to them before two of them hopped in the car and drove Raquel's body to the health clinic.

"You two need to decompress, so I'll have Jake drive you to the middle school." Squeezing Arianna's upper arm, he shook his head. "I'm so sorry. Another life wasted because of Luthor Cromwell's malice."

"Thank you," Arianna said quietly.

"Take today to mourn and bury Raquel, and then we can meet at sunrise to discuss next steps. I wish you had more time, but if Luthor's truly planning to attack, we need to prepare."

"I'm a soldier and have seen my share of death," Arianna said. "I'm heartbroken, but I understand the need to prevent more bloodshed."

"You two can hop in," Jake said, motioning them toward a small sedan.

When they were back at the school, Arianna listlessly headed to the makeshift room she'd claimed when they arrived at the compound. It was the former principal's office and had a large couch. Dominic followed her, determined to comfort her after the disastrous night.

She kicked off her boots and removed her pants before sitting on the couch and looking at her arm. "Fucker grazed me," she said, examining the wound.

"Be right back."

Dominic headed to the school's infirmary, noticing the first hints of dawn as they appeared outside the school windows. Retrieving some alcohol and a large bandage, he returned to Arianna.

Sitting beside her, he cleaned her wound and applied the bandage. As he worked, he noticed the flaring of her nostrils and the slight wobble of her chin as she grappled with the gravity that her sister was gone.

"Thanks," she muttered when he was finished, examining the bandage. "I should be fine with some rest." Releasing a defeated breath, she spread out on the couch and turned to face the wall. Reaching for the blanket that rested nearby, she tugged it up to her chin and closed her eyes.

Dominic removed everything but his underwear and slid in behind her. Drawing her close, he aligned his front with her back.

"You don't have to stay in here," she said, nuzzling into him as her body sent a message opposite of her words.

"You lost your sister today," he said, kissing her neck. "Of course I'm going to comfort you."

"I don't think I'm concussed even though I'm going to have one hell of a headache." She rubbed her temple. "How about you?"

"I think I'm fine too. Maverick will wake us up to debrief when he hears we're home, so I think it's fine if we get a few hours of sleep."

Nodding, she settled in as he tightened his arms around her. Her breathing was ragged as she fought off tears. He knew she rarely cried, but the day's events would spur emotion in even the most stoic soul.

"You're not alone anymore, sweetheart," he said, gently running his lips over the skin where her hair met her neck. "I thought you were finally ready to accept that."

"I've been alone for so long..." she trailed off, her voice laced with exhaustion.

Dominic held her, allowing his firm embrace to reaffirm his support.

"And don't call me 'sweetheart.'"

A laugh escaped his throat. Thankful to see a sliver of her acerbic personality shine through, Dominic closed his eyes, intent on holding her for as long as she needed.

Chapter 29

Arianna awoke, groggy and melancholy at her terrible failure to accomplish her goal. Sitting up, she rubbed the swollen bags under her eyes, noting that Dominic must've already risen. After tossing on some clothes, she headed to the home economics room, following the scent of bacon.

Dominic's broad shoulders stood at the stove as he flipped the bacon. Dani sat on Maverick's lap at the table, crying softly against his shoulder as he held her.

"Hey, guys," Arianna said, awkwardly scratching her arm beneath the bandage since she was uncomfortable with the display of emotion.

"Ari!" Dani cried, pushing to her feet and rushing toward her. After enveloping Arianna in a smothering hug, she drew back and studied the bandage. "Dominic said you were shot. Do I need to look at it?"

"Just grazed," Arianna said, squeezing her before releasing the hug. "I'm fine."

Dani gazed at her with red-rimmed eyes. "I can't believe she's gone."

"Me neither." Emotion clogged her throat. "I had one job and I fucking blew it."

"Hey," Maverick said, striding over and placing a supportive hand on Arianna's back. "That's the last time I want to hear that this was your fault. Raquel made her choices, and you put yourself in extreme danger to help her. We're happy you and Dom are okay."

Dominic sat the bacon on the table. "Eat while it's hot, guys."

The four of them sat, sad and solemn as they ate. Eventually, Arianna straightened her shoulders and spoke. "I want to bury her on the hill behind the school."

"The nurses are preparing her body, and Arthur is having his men make a casket," Dani said. "Burying her on the hill is perfect. She would've loved the little flowers that grow there, and hopefully her soul can find some peace there."

Arianna nodded. "After the burial, the three of us need to gather with Arthur's soldiers and form a plan." She pointed between herself, Dominic and Maverick. "Luthor is coming, and we need to brief everyone on the enhanced soldier serum, the rebellion and everything else we know."

"I wish I knew what was in the serum," Dani said, leaning her elbow on the table and resting her chin on her hand. "If I did, I could possibly concoct something to combat it."

"Raquel said there was something in it called…bromite?" Dominic asked, unsure.

"Bromantane?" Dani asked. "That's a performance-enhancing drug, so that makes sense."

"Well, let's find out." Arianna reached into her pocket and pulled out two vials. Setting them on the table, she cocked an eyebrow.

"Holy shit." Dani picked up a vial and lifted it to the light, studying it. "Where did you get this?"

"I stuffed two vials in my pocket before Zayne took us into custody in Dr. Ziegler's lab. I'm not a complete idiot," she said, playfully rolling her eyes.

"Damn, that's badass," Dominic said, reaching over and squeezing her hand. "I didn't even think to nab one of the vials."

"I'll do the thinking in this relationship, thank you very much," Arianna teased, squeezing his fingers.

Dani exchanged an excited glance with Maverick, beaming as Arianna huffed and stood. "Let it go, Dani. We like each other and he's fun to blow off steam with. That's all."

Dominic raised his hand to his mouth and whispered loudly, "She's crazy about me."

Dani chuckled as Arianna walked to the sink, refusing to get drawn into the lovey-dovey bullshit. "Want me to wash the pan?"

"I'll do it," Maverick said. "Why don't you and Dani take a walk and catch up? Dom, we can do the same."

"I'd like that," Dani said, rising. "We can remember her before we lay her to rest."

"Fine with me. After the funeral, I'll be ready to move on. Things are on a path now we can't change, and I'm ready to take on Luthor and end this shit."

"There's a cabin calling her name on a remote mountain in West Virginia somewhere," Dominic said, pointing his thumb over his shoulder at her.

"Only *her* name?" Maverick asked conspiratorially.

"I'm working on it, man. Give me some time."

Done with the annoying conversation, Arianna beckoned to Dani. "Let's head outside. I need some air."

Lacing her arm around Dani's waist, they left the men behind to reminisce about their sister and simpler times when none of the Lawson sisters needed to save the world.

Chapter 30

Hours later, they stood on the grassy hill, surrounded by the soulful songs of chirping birds in the nearby trees. Dani and Arianna were shoulder to shoulder, Maverick and Dominic positioned at their sides, solemn and supportive. The ceremony was reverent, each of them speaking kind words about Raquel as the cool breeze ruffled the fallen autumn leaves.

"I'm sorry you didn't get to say your last goodbye to Mom," Dani said, swiping away a tear as they stood by the raised pile of earth that covered her casket. "Hopefully she's with you now and you can hug her in all the ways you need."

Arianna slid an arm around her shoulders. "We failed you, and I'm sorry for that. But you can bet that I'll avenge you. Even though you pissed the hell out of me, you're my baby sister and that bastard will pay."

Embracing, they slowly swayed in tandem with the wind, their love evident as Dani rested her head on Arianna's shoulder.

When the ceremony was finished, Dani took Arianna's hand. "Remember I said I wanted to show you my progress on the antidote?"

"Yes. I need some good fucking news for once. I'm counting on you."

Grinning, Dani led the four of them to the red-brick clinic building, excitement pulsing deep in her belly. After climbing the stairs to the second floor, Arianna's eyes grew wide as she scanned the room.

Several patients were up and about, maneuvering on walkers as nurses helped them. Others sat playing chess or cards in the far corner.

Arianna slowly turned to face her sister, excitement in her eyes. "Holy shit," she breathed, her breath quickening slightly. "You created a cure."

Dani gripped her forearms, unable to control her smile. "You're goddamned right I created a cure."

Later that evening, Dani peered into the microscope, studying the serum Arianna had absconded from the lab.

"As Raquel said, it contains bromantane, and creatine too. The best way to counteract this is to create a serum from fungi that increases immune modulation."

"I've learned her language by now," Maverick said to Arianna, leaning on the counter behind them in the old middle school science lab. "In English, that means she can use mushrooms to create something we can inject into the super soldiers that will render them ineffective."

"Great job," Dani said, flashing him a grin. "Some of the *Agaricus* and turkey tail mushrooms I saw on our scouting trips around the compound should do it."

Arthur Reyes stormed into the room, causing them all to bristle.

"My lookouts just spotted a battalion of Sen Force soldiers marching toward the compound," he said, a steely determination in his eyes. "My men are ready."

"What's your current count?" Arianna asked, striding toward him.

"Ninety-seven. I wish we had more, but they're strong and committed soldiers who will fight with honor."

Maverick tugged Dani into a passionate kiss. "Stay inside the school. If the compound is infiltrated, head to the old basement gym locker rooms and lock yourself in."

"Be safe," she said, rising to her toes to peck his lips before releasing him. "I can't lose you too."

He nodded, his arms tightening into one last soulful embrace. Releasing her, he addressed Arthur. "Let's go."

"We'll arm ourselves and meet you at the front gate," Arianna said.

"Although we're outnumbered, our contingent is fierce and determined," Arthur said with a firm nod. "No one's infiltrating my compound without a fight."

Admiring his conviction, Arianna saluted him before treading toward her room to don her weapons, with Dominic fast on her heels.

Walking with purpose, she understood the gravity of the situation. Whether they were ready or not, the first battle in the war Tristan so desperately wanted was about to begin.

Chapter 31

Arianna strapped on every weapon she could fit onto her body. A knife in her boot, a gun at her waist and a rifle across her shoulder. Adding another gun on her opposite hip for good measure, she looked at Dominic. He was also loaded with weapons atop his black clothing, and she took a moment to peruse his body. Fuck, he was hot, and he was hers. If they survived, that was.

Determined to make that happen, she lifted her chin. "Ready?"

Approaching her, he lifted her chin and pressed a firm kiss to her lips. "You checking me out, Lawson?"

"Yeah." The corner of her lips ticked up. "Don't get hurt because I plan to personally remove those weapons from your body when we're done."

Desire lit his dark eyes. "I love your promises, sweetheart."

She nipped his lips, a small punishment for the endearment she swore she hated but also made butterflies flutter inside her stomach.

They marched to meet Arthur's militia, ready to fight for justice against a malicious dictator and his virulent drug.

Bootsteps pounded the ground as they approached the compound gates, and Arthur addressed the two lookouts perched at the top of the wall on either side.

"They're scattered throughout the woods, sir," one lookout said. "Armed with rifles and a few tanks."

"They underestimate us if they think I haven't trained our militia to fight in the forest in anticipation of this scenario," Arthur said, swinging the rifle around and clutching the grip. "You have the dart guns?" he asked the man in charge of the EverLife battalion.

"Locked and loaded, sir."

The EverLife battalion, comprised of fifteen men, had one job: to lodge darts full of EverLife into the Sen Force soldiers' necks. The compound's EverLife stock was diluted with all sorts of nefarious substances, which made it a perfect weapon. The darts were filled with three times the normal dose and would immobilize the Sen Force soldiers as soon as it entered the bloodstream.

Arthur ordered the gates to open, and urged everyone through them quickly so the people inside could remain protected. Arianna rushed outside, rifle held high as she scanned the surrounding trees.

A man stepped forward from the brush, the Sen Force patch on his shoulder glistening in the moonlight.

"I know him from working with Colonel McGrath," Arianna whispered to Dominic, who stood beside her in the formation.

"I'm Lieutenant Colonel Jackson," the man said, his voice cool and confident. "We've come here in peace to retake this compound for General Luthor Cromwell so he can evolve it into the next Sen City."

"We do not want your occupation, nor do we believe Cromwell has good intentions," Arthur called. "We believe his goal is ultimate destruction of our compound, and we won't allow that to happen."

"If you choose to fight, know that you are outnumbered. We have more ammunition than you can imagine and five tanks ready to fire at your compound walls." He pointed toward the thick metal grate surrounding the compound. "Although you melted down steel to fashion the wall, it won't survive a barrage by our tanks."

Arthur straightened his shoulders as his fingers tightened on his rifle. "No? We're prepared to test their readiness. To honor the rules of engagement, I'll warn you that I'm ten seconds away from commanding my men to fire."

Lieutenant Colonel Jackson sighed and shook his head. "Have it your way. If you want to die, I won't stop you—"

"Five seconds," Arthur said firmly.

Jackson backed into the brush seconds before Arthur yelled, "Attack!"

Arianna lurched forward, adrenaline in her veins as she ran toward a cluster of soldiers she spotted in a thicket of trees. Dominic was close behind her, his presence comforting in a way that had become routine. For a lone wolf like Arianna, the realization that she never wanted to fight another battle without him by her side hit hard.

And somehow, it was also the most heartening realization of her life.

Dominic swerved beside her, bullets flying from his rifle as they aimed at the Sen Force soldiers. Arianna ducked behind a thick tree, and Dominic followed close behind as he panted.

"Three down in that cluster, but there's another one at two o'clock with four men."

"Saw them," Arianna said with a nod. "I'll take the left flank."

Dominic gave a quick tilt of his head and they were off, emerging from the thicket and spraying bullets at the soldiers. A loud boom signaled behind them, followed by a flash of fire, and Arianna ducked.

"They're firing at the walls!" Dominic yelled, his breath ragged as he surveyed the nearby thicket. "That cluster is down. We need to take out the tanks."

Arianna jogged toward two fallen Sen Force soldiers and lifted the huge weapon from one man's lifeless frame. "Look what I found," she whispered, excitement in her tone.

"A rocket propelled grenade," Dominic said, eyeing the weapon. "It's the only weapon that could possibly destroy the tanks."

"Exactly," she said with a nod. "We need to approach the tank from behind since that's the most vulnerable spot. Hopefully, it will work. It's still going to be tough."

"Lead the way." Dominic's spine straightened with resolve as he prepared to follow her.

They jogged through the trees and foliage, the tank that was firing upon the wall an eerie sight in the dense woods outside the compound. The sounds of bullets and combat filled Arianna's ears as she kneeled behind a large rock and aimed the RPG.

Dominic crouched beside her, rifle aimed as he waited.

The tank exploded in a huge blaze, the ammunition inside igniting a destructive force that would leave no survivors.

"Good shot," Dominic said. "Let's move to the next tank.

They skulked through the woods, eventually locating another tank whose barrel was aimed at the compound wall. It wasn't firing so Arianna ducked behind a tree to observe it, wondering if the barrel was malfunctioning somehow.

Suddenly, the top of the hatch opened and three men climbed out, the Sen Force patch slightly visible on their uniforms in the darkened forest.

"I'm the tank commander," one man said, holding up his hands in a sign of surrender. "My gunner, driver and I have no wish to die tonight. We pledged loyalty to Luthor to feed our families. We know you have an RPG and don't want this to escalate further between us."

Arianna glanced at Dominic as the three soldiers stood silent, hands raised as they waited.

"Let's take them hostage and question them. They can give us Sen Force intel."

"Get on your knees and cross your wrists behind your back," she commanded. The soldiers complied, and Arianna placed two fingers between her lips, whistling to two of Arthur's men a few yards away. "Restrain these soldiers and tie them to a tree. When the dust settles, we'll take them inside the compound for questioning."

The men nodded and rushed toward them, securing their wrists before leading them into the forest.

"Should we move to the next tank?" she asked, arching her eyebrows.

"Absolutely," Dominic said. "It's interesting to see some of the soldiers wavering in their support of Luthor. It's a good sign."

They maneuvered through the woods, searching for the next tank when Arianna's ears perked. Surprise coursed through her when she heard someone yell, "Cease fire!"

Treading back to the compound entrance, she observed Arthur kneeling over Lieutenant Colonel Jackson as he heaved atop the ground.

"You've got a dart full of shitty EverLife in your neck, Jackson," he said, shaking his head. "It will stop your heart soon. I've called a ceasefire and need you to affirm it to your men. The ones still alive don't have to die today."

Ragged breaths formed visible puffs in the chilly air as Jackson contemplated. Turning his head atop the wet leaves, he spoke to the man Arianna assumed was his second-in-command.

"I've pledged my life to Luthor's cause and want to die with honor. This is in your hands now, son." Shallow breaths left his lungs as the drug continued to poison his blood. "May God be with you." Jackson's head lolled on the ground as his heart succumbed to the drug. His muscles convulsed in a series of spasms before he exhaled and his body fell limp.

The second-in-command lifted his gaze to Arthur's, indecision swimming in his dark eyes. Squaring his shoulders, he raised his hand high and yelled, "Charge!"

Arthur rose and sprinted toward a nearby thicket, commanding his men to regroup. Once they were gathered in the thick brush, he spoke between labored breaths.

"Spread the Sen Force soldiers out across the woods and shoot to wound, not kill. If we have enough soldiers bleeding out on the dirt, I can try and convince the new commander to surrender and offer to heal the wounded."

Arianna thought it was a solid strategy. Immobilize one by one until the enemy was fractured. Noticing that some of the men were hesitating, she stood tall and addressed Arthur. "Solid plan, sir. Dominic and I will take the east woods. You two, come with us," she commanded, pointing to the two closest soldiers.

Arthur's gaze drilled into hers as he nodded, silently thanking her for her support.

Arianna led their small group onto a nearby dirt path as others clustered together, each spreading out across different sectors of the forest.

"He needed that affirmation from you in front of the soldiers," Dominic said softly as they stepped through the brush, weapons lifted while they scanned for Sen Force soldiers. "Like I've said all along, we have a chance because of you, Arianna."

Tamping down the emotion that swelled at his unwavering belief in her, she shot him a glance. "Let's take down some soldiers first and see if we have a chance."

White teeth flashed under the stars as he grinned. "Yes, ma'am."

Confident with him by her side, Arianna trekked in the darkness, determined to make this battle count and change the course of the world for those who no longer had the ability to fight.

Chapter 32

Arianna crept through the woods, slowly wounding soldiers with shots to their thighs and arms as the night progressed. Arthur had been smart to train his men in the forest, and they were much more skilled at combat in the dense brush than Luthor's army.

Eventually, the horizon began to glow a slight eerie gray, and a whistle sounded in the distance. Glancing toward Dominic, who was crouched behind the cluster of bushes to her left, she lifted her eyebrows in a silent question.

He rose and strode toward her, positioning himself beside her as they stood in the shadow of protection of a large oak tree. "I think it's Arthur calling us back," he said, jerking his head toward the sound of the whistle.

"Agreed. Stay alert. There could still be stragglers who haven't been wounded."

They slowly made their way back to the clearing in front of the compound gates. Arthur stood tall, his gun aimed at the man Lieutenant Colonel Jackson had transferred command to before he died. Blood trickled from the man's upper arm as one of Arthur's men held him immobile.

"I can shoot you right here, son," Arthur said, the barrel of his gun aimed between the man's eyes. "Or we can talk like two commanders who want what's best for our troops."

A wail sounded in the distance, and Arianna assumed it was one of the Sen Force soldiers who'd been wounded, crying as he bled out on the forest floor.

"You're young, and I understand your desire to fight for your convictions," Arthur continued. "But your convictions are misplaced. Luthor Cromwell is not a just leader."

"And you are?" the man asked, his voice laced with pain from the wound in his arm.

Lowering his gun, Arthur stepped forward. "What is your name, soldier? I owe you the honor of addressing you properly."

The commander swallowed visibly before answering. "Major Anthony Martinez," he said, eyes darting to the sound of another wail that echoed off the far horizon.

"My sister's husband was named Anthony," Arthur said, his lips forming a sad smile. "We called him Tony. He and my sister both died from EverLife addiction."

Anthony's chest lifted with slow breaths as he contemplated. "My family called me Tony too. Those that are left still do, but there aren't many."

Compassion laced Arthur's features as he slowly extended his hand. "I'm very sorry to hear that. Although I'm technically Commander Reyes, you can call me Arthur. Can I call you Tony?"

Tony grasped his hand, giving a slow, wary shake. "Yes."

Arthur studied him as he contemplated. "Is this truly the service you signed up for, Tony? Willful alliance to a demagogue who controls the world with an addictive, poisonous drug?"

Tony's eyes lowered as his shoulders sagged. "No, sir. But the world has changed, and we must make hard choices to ensure our survival."

"So let's change it back." Arthur released his hand and took a step forward. "In fact, let's change it for the better. A world worthy of your children."

"I don't have children yet, sir, but I hope to one day."

"Then let's create something together," he said, a slight plea in his voice, alongside the firm strength. "If you're willing to discuss forming an alliance with me, Tony, I'll invite you inside to talk. In exchange, I'll send my nurses out here to tend to your wounded soldiers."

Tony's lips pursed as he contemplated.

"Aligning against Luthor Cromwell is impossible," Tony said. "He controls the entire army. The entire *world*."

The corner of Arthur's lips ticked up. "For now. But his confidence might be his downfall. I doubt he'll suspect that your battalion has formed a secret alliance with us. If we're strategic, we could turn this into an insurmountable advantage."

Tony deliberated for a small eternity as birds ushered in the day with soulful songs from the nearby trees. Another cry sounded in the distance before a gunshot reverberated in the forest with a loud bang.

Tony shuddered at the sound as Arthur shook his head. "That man didn't have to die, Tony. How many more have to die? Please..." Extending his hand, he held up his palm. "Let me send my nurses out and come inside the walls to talk. I promise you no harm will befall you."

Tony tilted his head back and closed his eyes, and Arianna wondered if he was praying. Finally, he refocused his gaze on Arthur and lifted his hand in a salute. "Sir, I will accompany you inside if you send out your nurses."

Relief washed over Arthur's face as he saluted in return.

"Cease fire!" Tony called to what remained of his troops. "I've agreed to accompany Commander Reyes inside the compound in exchange for triage. Do not engage. Understood?"

"Yes, sir!"

"Gather the nurses and have them triage the men," Arthur commanded to the soldier who stood behind him. Stepping back, he gestured toward the front gates of the compound. "After you, Tony."

Arianna exhaled a heavy breath, releasing the tension in her weary muscles. Dominic cupped her shoulder and squeezed, silently affirming his relief as well. Lifting her gaze to his, a smile tugged at her lips as a small sliver of the optimism she so rarely felt coursed through her veins.

They were a long way from victory, but perhaps they were a few steps closer.

Sliding her arm around Dominic's waist, she pressed into his side as they walked back to the compound.

CHAPTER 33

An hour later, Arianna stood inside the hub of Arthur's compound as he questioned Tony. The man was talking rather freely, and she understood how many soldiers had been forced to comply with Luthor's orders due to necessity. Hopefully, Arthur would end up being the leader they needed; one who would restore society to something better. Perhaps even something whole.

"Do you know Zayne Danvers's location?" Arthur asked, leg swinging as he sat on the table, arms crossed as he questioned Tony, seated a foot away.

Tony shook his head. "We think he's being funded by George Luddington, but we're not sure. George disappeared after Luthor was injured, and Luthor has sent a search team to find him. He sent two separate teams to search Zayne and Tristan Holder. We don't think they're working together...yet."

"And Zayne is holding Luthor's wife hostage?"

"Yes. Grace was abducted the night Luthor was hurt. His desire to save her stems more from not wanting to look weak than affection, if you want my opinion. The most powerful man in the world can't have his wife murdered. Not a good look." He shrugged dismissively.

"It certainly isn't." Arthur looked toward Arianna, Dominic and Maverick. "Anything else you want to ask him?"

"I think I'm good," Arianna said. "The plan to send Tony and his troops back with Jackson's body, claiming defeat, is solid. This will cause Luthor to regroup, but he won't know Tony's secretly on our side."

Arthur nodded. "In the meantime, I'd like to send my own team to search for Zayne and Tristan. It's time for us all to unite against Luthor. Rebels, soldiers, militia—I don't care what we call it, but we're more powerful together."

"I pledge my loyalty to you, sir, and will do my best to honor our alliance," Tony said.

"You've done a good job, son. I hope this doesn't sound condescending, but I'm proud of you. Your actions today could very well pave the way for peace and are extremely meaningful."

Arthur stood and patted Tony on the shoulder as the younger soldier's shoulders straightened with pride. "We'll make sure to protect your family and all the citizens we can when we forge our attack. A clean, precise mission is best, and we'll try our damndest." He gestured to the door. "For now, my team has packed up some food for your troops. We don't have a lot to spare, but give it to your families when you return to DC. I'll communicate with you on the radio frequency we discussed."

Tony stood and extended his hand. "I was only a kid when you declared your intention to run for president, but I think I would've voted for you, sir."

Arthur shook his hand as his lips formed a sincere smile. "Maybe you'll have the chance one day. I appreciate your service, Tony."

Tony pivoted, following the team members who would lead him to the packed food.

"What a fucking day," Arthur said, scraping his hands over his face. "I'm beat."

"We need sleep too," Dominic said. "But I just want to say, you're a fantastic leader, Reyes. I'm honored to serve with you."

"Me too," Arianna said.

Grinning, Arthur tilted his head. "The great Arianna Lawson has finally accepted me. I'm humbled."

He bowed dramatically, and Arianna rolled her eyes. "Don't let it go to your head. Also, can we get a fucking bed in the principal's office? I'm tired of sleeping on a couch."

Chuckling, he hooked his fingers to call one of his men over. "There's a couch with a pull-out bed in my quarters. Move it to the principal's office at the middle school."

"On it," the man said, waving two others to follow him to Arthur's downstairs quarters.

"They'll have it there in twenty minutes and it's the best I can do."

"We'll take it."

Arthur raised his eyebrows, a knowing smile on his face.

"For sleeping," she said, exasperated. "Everyone is a goddamn matchmaker around here. I'm going to bed."

She stomped from the room, ignoring Arthur's chuckles behind her as they mingled with Dominic's and Maverick's before they followed her outside.

They briskly walked to the school under the early morning sky, and when they entered, Dani ran toward them. "Is everyone okay? What happened?"

"I'll tell you everything, slugger," Maverick said, sliding his arm around her waist. "We're exhausted, and I'm sure Arianna and Dom are ready to crash."

Three men busted through the double doors, carrying a couch and echoing hellos as they passed.

"I needed a bed," Arianna said, rubbing her tense neck. "I'm done with the couch."

"Plus, it will give you two more room," Dani said with a cheeky grin.

Arianna groaned before walking away. "Good night!" she said, flicking a dismissive hand as she disappeared down the hallway.

Dominic wished them good night as well before his footsteps sounded behind her. Knowing he would soon be wrapped around her was not only comforting, it felt *right*. She entered the principal's office, noticing the men putting sheets on the pull-out mattress.

"Grabbed a clean set of bedding from Arthur's closet," one of them said. "You should be all set. We moved the old couch against the far wall, but we can remove it if you need."

"Nope, we're good. Thanks, guys." Arianna watched them leave, the door clicking behind them before Dominic turned the deadbolt.

"What a fucking night," he said, trailing toward her and cupping her chin. "Are you okay?"

"Yes." Rising to her toes, she brushed his lips with hers before extricating herself from his grasp so they could remove their weapons. They placed them on the desk, one by one, before Arianna slipped her hand in his.

Lacing their fingers, she drew him to the center of the room atop the withered green carpet. Overcome with every emotion she felt for him, she lowered to her knees.

A visible shudder ran down his frame, causing her body to ripple with delight. Inching closer, he slid his fingers under her chin, tilting her head back. "Ari..."

"I think it's time to make some of those fantasies come true," she whispered before darting her tongue over her lips. Passion flared in his eyes, and her heart pounded at the glow of admiration across his strong features.

"You don't have to," he murmured, tracing his thumb over her wet bottom lip. "I know you're tired."

Reaching for his fly, she gazed into his eyes as she unbuttoned his pants and lowered the zipper. "I *want* to," she rasped, pushing the fabric away. "I'm filled with adrenaline and I need a fucking release. But if you want to punish me for not letting you sleep, I'm okay with that."

A long, desire-laden breath filtered through his lungs as her fingers fought to free him. "Fuck, you're perfect. You know that, right?" Palming her jaw, he ran his thumb over her cheek. "So goddamned perfect."

Arianna dragged his pants and boxer briefs down his legs until they scrunched above his boots. His shaft surged toward her, thick and turgid, the veins pulsing beneath the sensitive skin. Sliding her fingers around his length, she squeezed, thrilled at his sharp inhale.

He cupped her head, threading his fingers through the hair beneath her braid. Resting the smooth head of his cock on her lips, he softly commanded, "Open that smart mouth, Ari."

She complied, opening wide and gasping when he surged inside. He slowly began to pump between her lips, his hands holding her head firm as he stared into her eyes.

"Such a gorgeous mouth," he rasped, dragging his length back and forth over her tongue...between her lips...coating himself in her saliva as he undulated. "*My mouth*, Ari. Do you hear me?"

She nodded, feeling her eyes water as he pushed deeper, hitting the back of her throat with each solid thrust.

"Is it too much?" he asked, his deep orbs swirling with lust and emotion.

She shook her head, gripping the base of his cock and stroking it as he surged inside her mouth. God, it felt so good to have him loom above her. To know he was now a constant in her life. Gazing into his eyes, she squeezed the base of his shaft and popped him from her mouth.

"You can go harder," she said, her tone silky as she stroked his wet flesh. "I meant it when I said you could punish me." She'd never considered offering that level of submission to any man, but for Dom? Fuck, she wanted his hands everywhere—craved his marks on her skin. She wanted him to *claim* her.

Cursing, he kicked off his boots and pants, tossing them aside. Lifting her under the arms, he carried her to the bed and threw her on the mattress face-first. Laughing at the exhilaration of finally fucking someone stronger than her, she rested on her elbows as he ripped off the rest of their clothes. Hoping to entice him, she lifted her ass in the air, wriggling as he uttered a deep groan.

"Were you laughing?" he grumbled, gripping one globe of her ass in each hand and squeezing.

Nodding, she bit her lip. "You're the first man who's ever tossed me around in bed. I love that you're stronger than me—"

"No one's stronger than you" was his soft reply as he leaned forward and whispered in her ear. "You're the strongest person I've ever known, Ari."

Tears stung her eyes at the heartfelt words. "I meant physically."

Cold air washed over her ass cheek before she felt a sharp sting. Her body lurched forward as pleasure coursed through her frame.

"Mine," he gritted, his palm crashing against her burning skin yet again. His palm whacked her ass before he smoothed it, causing moisture to rush between her thighs.

"*Oh god...*" she moaned, squirming atop the comforter. "Do the other one."

His deep chuckle surrounded her as he began to smack her other cheek. Closing her eyes, Arianna gave in to the pleasure as wetness gushed down her inner thighs. To say she'd never been so aroused was an understatement.

"Look at this glistening pussy," he murmured, gripping her ass and spreading her wide. Placing two fingers against her core, he dragged them back and forth over her quivering folds. "Tell me to fuck you."

"Good lord, fuck me," she cried, clenching the covers. "I didn't think you needed an invitation at this point—"

His cock slammed inside her, filling every crevice as he aligned his chest with her back. The tiny hairs on his pecs scratched the sensitive skin of her upper back, the sensation adding to the sense of fullness from having his hard cock so deep inside her.

"I'm going to fuck you so deep you feel me in your bones," he rasped, jutting inside her with forceful strokes, the tip of his cock hitting the spot deep within that no one else ever had.

"I didn't think I could come this way..." she moaned, her fingers gripping the bed so hard she thought they might crack. "Not until you..."

"Because you were made for me, Ari," he grunted, maintaining the maddening pace as he stimulated her G-spot with every thrust.

Stars exploded behind her eyelids as she opened wider, aching for everything he could give her.

"There's my good girl." Warm breath flitted around the shell of her ear, the praise sending a jolt of elation through her frame and a fresh gush of arousal to douse his cock.

"I'm close," she whimpered, barely able to speak as the orgasm loomed on the horizon. "Fuck, Dom...it's *so good*..."

He groaned, resting more weight on her as he continued the deep, maddening strokes. Resting his forehead against her temple, he bit her earlobe, sending her headlong into a blistering climax.

Deep convulsions ripped through her core—deeper than she'd ever felt—and her spasming muscles dragged him deeper, choking his cock as he breathed her name.

"So fucking tight," he moaned, sweat dripping from his body to coat hers as she drowned in the abyss. "You're draining me...*oh god*...I can't stop it..."

He exploded seconds after pulling out, coating her lower back with pulsing jets of release. Overcome with pleasure and elation at how free she felt with him, she began to laugh, the sound joyous as her body quaked underneath his. Burying his face in her neck, he gripped her shoulders, searching for a stronghold. His strong frame trembled as he sighed her name, his body shuddering with every pulse. When he was finally spent, he collapsed against her, breathing labored huffs in her ear as she giggled beneath.

"Good grief, you're giggling," he droned, rubbing his nose against the sensitive skin behind her ear. "Since when do you giggle?"

"Since you fucked me senseless," she murmured, the words garbled since her cheek was pressed against the bed. "I usually need my clit...you know...but you got it done. I can't really talk right now, but you get the gist."

"I know." Placing a sweet peck on her nape, he sank into her, slowly relaxing as they recovered. "It's all part of my master plan to make you fall madly in love with me."

"Is that so?" she teased, aware of how the organ in her chest slammed at his words.

"Mmm hmm."

Lying there, entwined in sweaty, sated bliss, she debated telling him she'd loved him as long as she'd known him. Deciding her brain was too mushy and she wasn't quite ready, she relaxed and snuggled into him instead.

His calloused palm trailed lazily over her still-stinging butt cheek, and she smiled at the possessive yet tender strokes. "You really went for it with the spanking, Dom. Geez."

Full lips curved against her nape. "Did you like it?"

"Oh, hell yes. And I liked sucking you too. Next time, I'll let you deep throat me."

His sated shaft jerked against her back, causing her to snicker. "Guess your dick likes that idea too."

"Oh, yeah, he likes it," Dominic murmured, kissing a trail from her neck to her ear. "And I've seen you swim in the pond behind the school, so I know how long you can hold your breath. Lucky me."

Tossing back her head, she broke into harmonious laughter, unable to squelch the joy of being in his arms. His deep laughter entwined with hers, and for one moment, Arianna allowed herself to be blissfully, unapologetically happy.

A blunt finger tapped her neck, and she turned her head to stare into those deep eyes.

"Yes?"

His gaze was intense as he cupped her jaw, gently stroking her cheek as he swallowed thickly. Was he...nervous?

"I want to come inside you when we do this, Ari. No more pulling out and no more condoms."

Her eyes widened as she digested the words. "I can't fight if I'm pregnant, Dom."

"Then I'll fight for you."

Swallowing the lump in her throat, she shook her head. "I can't put that burden on you. You need me. Dani needs me. The *cause* needs me."

Strong fingers stroked her cheek as he spoke in a low, soothing tone. "I desperately need you, but you also deserve to be happy. You'll be forty soon, and tomorrows are never guaranteed in this world."

"Thanks for the reminder I'm washed up," she teased, rolling her eyes.

Dominic breathed a laugh. "We're both washed up, and that means we've lived long enough to know that we have to seize happiness." He brushed a tender kiss across her lips. "Let me give you a baby, sweetheart." His expression was so genuine it almost shattered her heart. "I want to give you everything."

Flattening her lips, she struggled to keep the tears that clouded her eyes from falling. "Dominic," she whispered, slowly shaking her head on the mattress. "This is a huge decision."

"What decision? Between me or the turkey baster? I'm really hoping I have a slight edge in that competition." He squished his features, looking adorable as he waited for her answer.

Exhaling a long breath, she shifted and pulled him closer. Gliding her leg over his thigh, she contemplated him, struggling to control the heartbeat that pulsed in every cell of her body.

Cupping his jaw, she stroked her thumb over his lips. "If you give me a baby, I'm going to want forever. And no one's ever lasted forever with me. I'm not sure I'm built for that."

"Bullshit." Gliding his palm over her ass, he squeezed. "You just haven't met anyone who's built to spend forever with you. Until me."

A stupid tear fell, making her feel clumsy and vulnerable as she tried to keep her emotions in check. "I'm not ready," she said, wondering when her voice had turned to gravel. "It's too much for me, Dom."

A smile tugged at the edges of his firm lips. "God, you're so pretty when you cry," he said, swiping the tear from her cheek.

Scoffing, she rolled her eyes. "I look like a punching bag when I cry. Most men would think it's gross."

"Which men? Because this man thinks you're stunning." He squeezed her ass again as he smiled. "And this man wants to have a baby with you." His other hand grazed over her cheek as his eyes bore into hers. "This man *loves* you,

Ari. If you won't say it, I'll say it. I don't want to be a shell of a person anymore. You make me want more."

Scattered breaths left her lungs as she digested his poignant words. "Dom…"

"It's okay, sweetheart," he said, drawing her close and pressing her face to his chest. "If you're not ready to say it, I'll say it for both of us until you are."

Chapter 34

D ominic held his strong, gorgeous woman as her body trembled against his chest. Suddenly, she began to cry, sobs racking her frame as she finally let emotion surge past her thick walls. Joy flooded every crevice of his body as he closed his eyes, soaking up all her past heartache and pain. Her breakdown was messy...and raw...and *glorious*, and he treasured the opportunity to finally support the woman who unselfishly supported everyone else.

"I've got you," he soothed, stroking her cooling skin as she shuddered in his arms. "Falling in love doesn't have to be a disaster."

"I swore I wasn't going to let this happen," she mumbled against his chest.

Chuckling at her stubbornness, he rubbed his chin atop her head. "Hard to believe two bastards like us fear something as basic as human emotion. But here we are."

"Speak for yourself," she said, lifting her head and swiping her arm under her nose. "I'm not a bastard. I'm practical."

"You're fucking terrified, Arianna. I'd chide you for it if I wasn't dead set on finishing this conversation and earning your trust." He slid his hand over her braid. "And seeing you open and vulnerable like this, knowing it's a side you rarely show, makes me feel like a goddamned superhero."

Wet eyes roved over his face, the hues of green and brown stunning in the small shaft of light from the lamp atop the desk. "You really do love me," she breathed.

An exasperated huff leapt from his throat. "Do you think I throw those words around often? Of course I love you, woman. How do you not know that?"

"Even though I drive you crazy half the time?"

Chuckling, he caressed her damp cheek. "*Because* you drive me crazy. You keep me on my toes and I need that. You present a challenge that I'll conquer every day if you let me."

Relaxing into the bed, she gazed up at him, licking her lips and jolting his cock as he mentally prepared for round two. *After* he'd consoled her, of course. She was opening up to him, but she was also pressed against him—sated and pliant—and he was only a man, after all.

"And you'd be happy living off the grid? I'm talking a cabin deep in the mountains where no one will bother us. Once we save the world, obviously."

Grinning, he nodded.

"It's not the most exciting life—"

Placing his fingers over her lips, he cut her off. "Every second with you is exciting, Ari. Infuriating and frustrating...but also very exciting," he finished with a wink.

Her wide smile shot a crack down the heart that she alone had repaired. The heart he'd reopened just for her.

"It won't be easy. We barely tolerate each other sometimes."

"Until we started fucking. Then you became pretty agreeable."

Narrowing her eyes, she muttered, "Idiot. Thinks his cock makes me agreeable."

Catching her off guard, he snaked over her body, drawing her arms above her head and securing them with one hand. Gently placing his other hand around her neck, he softly squeezed.

"This is the only way I want to strangle you anymore. With that luscious body beneath me as you scream my name."

Desire lit her eyes as she pushed into his hand. God, this woman would be his undoing. Her acquiescence to his dominance pushed every button embedded in his soul. He fucking loved knowing he was the only person in the world Arianna submitted to.

"And if you're not ready to say the words, I'll accept that. For now." He grazed a kiss across her lips. "But I'm going to give you a baby, Arianna. And we're going to raise it together on the side of some fucking mountain if that's what you want. Mark my words. Once we finish our mission, that's what I aim to accomplish."

The dash of vulnerability returned to her eyes, slight but noticeable as she swallowed thickly beneath his palm. "I'm afraid I won't make you happy. That I won't be...*enough* to make you stay. And it's hard for me to say that because I'm confident and it goes against my nature to doubt myself. But, with you, it's important I get it out there. I won't allow myself to enter into something that's going to fail. I've learned how painful that is and I won't do it again."

"Then we won't fail." Sliding his hand from her neck to her jaw, he stared into her eyes, showing her his resolve. "I think we can do anything as long as we do it together. And I think you do too."

"I had my doubts...but I'm coming around." Forming a sultry grin, she glided her calf over his hairy thigh. "And even though I'm a sticky mess and this has been the longest day in history, I think I have a small amount of energy left."

"Sleep is overrated," he muttered before pressing his lips to hers in a heated kiss.

Much later, when they lay sprawled on the bed after another round of epic lovemaking, Dominic held her atop his body as they panted from exertion.

"I'm too old for this," she mumbled against his chest. "You're not supposed to have the best sex of your life at forty."

"Am I the best you've ever had?" he asked, elated at the sentiment while simultaneously feeling his ego soar.

"By a damn longshot." Pressing her elbow into his chest, she rested her cheek on her fist.

"Better than the turkey baster?" Dominic teased.

"Asshole."

His deep laugh reverberated around them as he drew lazy patterns on her back. Suddenly, she slithered over him, cupping both of his cheeks as she gazed into his eyes.

"Fuck it," she whispered, shaking her head. "I'm tired of being scared too." Running her finger over his lips, she inhaled a shaky breath. "I love you, Dominic. I've loved you since you stepped on my toes at Dani's wedding."

His palm splayed across her lower back as he grinned. "I'm still going to make that up to you."

"I loved you when we started this mission together. I loved you that night we took the food to the kids by the campfire near the farmhouse."

"I think I loved you that night too," he said, running his knuckles over her jaw. "You were determined to help those kids, and I was determined to help *you*."

Her eyebrow arched. "It was annoying. I wanted to go by myself, but you're a stubborn son of a bitch."

His lips twitched before his gaze grew solemn. "I'm sorry I was too stupid to realize my feelings for you then. I'm sorry I hurt you, Arianna."

"I know." Nestling against him, she rested her cheek on his chest. "And I love you for saying that too."

"Well, it's pretty apparent we love each other. What do we do now?"

Her fingernails dug into his chest, directly over his heart, as if she were claiming it as her own. "We help Arthur and Dani save the world, have some babies and live happily ever after."

"And get married," he said, caressing her braid.

"Fine." She yawned, her voice growing sleepy as she relaxed against him. "But I don't need a ring. Just give me a gun or a weapon. Any weapon will suffice."

And that, Dominic thought as he curled his arms around her, was exactly why he loved Arianna Lawson. His brave, loyal soldier, and the woman who'd finally dragged him out of his self-imposed shell.

Holding her tight, he whispered promises in her ear as she drifted on his chest, knowing the rest of his life would be fuller just because she was in it.

Together, they would fight to free the world from oppression and addiction. When they succeeded, Dominic would finally build a life worthy of the one his sister and parents wished for him.

Because of Arianna, he would have the future he deserved.

Grateful, he vowed to love her in the way she should've always been loved: completely. Utterly. Forever.

A valiant oath for the amazing woman who would share the rest of his days by his side and deep in his heart.

Epilogue

Three weeks later

T ristan crept through the woods that surrounded the small cabin in rural Pennsylvania. Two soldiers marched behind him, both of whom had grudges against Luthor Cromwell. Tristan didn't necessarily consider them friends—after all, his social skills had been garbage since the world turned to shit and he'd become obsessed with killing Luthor. But they all shared the same cause, and that was enough for Tristan.

Glancing back, he made eye contact with both men, silently commanding them to follow. They approached the house, and Tristan tested the first stair with his toe, grimacing when it creaked.

Gesturing toward the door with his head, he indicated his intent to strike. Both men nodded, and Tristan forged ahead.

After cresting the rickety stairs, he kicked open the door, rifle clutched in his hands as he rushed inside.

"Hands up!" he called, quickly scanning the room. Two men stood by a desk at the far end of the room beside a blazing stone fireplace. Two more exited what he assumed was the kitchen, halting as their eyes grew wide.

The men by the desk faced him and drew their guns from their holsters. Tristan looked directly into Zayne Danver's eyes, shock pervading his system at the knowledge he'd finally located him.

Golden hair flashed beside Zayne as the woman behind the desk lifted her gaze to his, annoyance in the deep blue orbs. Tristan's heart lurched with relief that she was still alive.

"Grace," he breathed, walking slowly but purposefully toward her, unfazed by the men with guns aimed at his chest. "If you hurt her, I swear to god—"

"Tristan," she said, her voice calm beneath the ringing that raged in his ears. "Put the rifle down."

Clenching his teeth, he stopped two feet from the desk, aiming the barrel at Zayne's chest. "Let. Her. Go."

Zayne looked at Grace, eyebrows lifting as he seemed to silently ask her permission.

Sighing, she rose, her face an impassive mask as she approached Tristan. Drawing closer, she stopped only inches from him and placed her index finger on the rifle. Gently pushing it down, she leaned forward.

"What the hell are you doing?" she hissed.

Tristan's throat bobbed as confusion coursed through him. "I'm rescuing you."

A breathy laugh escaped her throat before she pinched the bridge of her nose in apparent frustration.

"My men and I can take them, Grace. Let me help you—"

"Stop talking," she interrupted.

"Grace—"

"You oblivious fool," she said, fire flashing in her gorgeous eyes. "Do I look like I need to be rescued?"

Bristling, he glanced around the room.

"You could never get out of your own way, Tristan. Still, after all this time." Stepping forward, she pushed his gun aside. Crowding his space, her scent overwhelmed him as she stared into his eyes.

"You daft man. I never needed saving. Don't you see?"

Tristan's eyes widened as realization finally clicked into place.

Thrusting her chin forward, she spoke with the regality of a queen and the strength of a warrior. "Darling, *I'm* the one leading the rebellion."

Before You Go

Well, lovely readers, I had to do it. If you've read my books or followed me for a while, you know I LOVE a good twist. And man, that one was a doozy, right? Who knew Grace had it in her? I hope you're as excited to discover the conclusion to this trilogy as I was when I envisioned this story arc and began writing it!

You can order Book 3 in the Sendaxa Chronicles trilogy, **Fated Salvation**, now! Our tortured, morally gray hero Tristan and rebellion leader Grace are going to try and find their happy ending while helping Dani, Maverick, Arianna and Dominic save the world. I hope they succeed!

Thank you for coming on this journey with me and loving these characters as much as I do. Arianna and Dominic are some of my favorite characters I've EVER written, and I adored writing their story. Wishing you lots of happy reading and may you continue to find YOUR HEA in this crazy, intense world we all inhabit together. Reading has always been an escape for me, and it warms my heart that you spend your time and money to escape with these characters I love too. –Rebecca

ALSO BY REBECCA HEFNER

The Sendaxa Chronicles
Book 1: Repressed Echoes
Book 2: Scorched Redemption
Book 3: Fated Salvation

Etherya's Earth Series
Prequel: The Dawn of Peace
Book 1: The End of Hatred
Book 2: The Elusive Sun
Book 3: The Darkness Within
Book 4: The Reluctant Savior
Book 4.5: Immortal Beginnings
Book 5: The Impassioned Choice
Book 5.5: Two Souls United
Book 6: The Cryptic Prophecy
Book 6.5: Garridan's Mate
Book 7: The Diplomatic Heir
Book 7.5: Sebastian's Fate
Book 8: The Solitary Protector

Prevent the Past Trilogy
Book 1: A Paradox of Fates
Book 2: A Destiny Reborn
Book 3: A Timeline Restored

ABOUT THE AUTHOR

USA Today bestselling author Rebecca Hefner grew up in Western NC and now calls the Hudson River of NYC home. In her youth, she would sneak into her mother's bedroom and read the romance novels stashed on the bookshelf, cementing her love of HEAs. A huge Buffy and Star Wars fan, she loves an epic fantasy and a surprise twist (Luke, he IS your father).

Before becoming an author, Rebecca had a successful twelve-year medical device sales career. After launching her own indie publishing company, she is now a full-time author who loves writing strong, complex characters who find their HEAs. Rebecca can usually be found making dorky and/or embarrassing posts on TikTok and Instagram. Please join her so you can laugh along with her!

www.ingramcontent.com/pod-product-compliance
Lightning Source LLC
Chambersburg PA
CBHW061819190726
48289CB00007B/2249